# BAD TIMING

## Owanna De St Jeor

A Judy Sullivan Book

Walker and Company
New York

First published in the United States of America
in 1984 by the Walker Publishing Company, Inc.

Published simultaneously in Canada by John Wiley & Sons
Canada, Limited, Rexdale, Ontario.

De St Jeor, Owanna, 1926-
   Bad timing.

   "A Judy Sullivan book."
   I. Title.
PS3554.E1158B3      1984          813'.54          83-40425
ISBN: 0-8027-0774-2

Printed in the United States of America

10  9  8  7  6  5  4  3  2  1

# Chapter One

ERIKA WHEATLY WALKED through the door to her drab office and flopped in the chair at her desk, heaving a sigh. "What a day," she groaned. Lifting a silky strand of blonde hair from her cheek, she twisted it around her index finger as the image of the woman lying in a hospital bed continued to skitter through her mind. In an attempt to vanquish the persistent vision, once more she spoke aloud to the empty room. "I simply can't believe today. What a bummer." Her deep blue eyes scanned the room and rested on the wall clock. It was after four, too soon to leave and too late to begin something important. Reaching for a stack of papers and wrinkling her nose in distaste, she began to sort them, place them in folders and arrange the folders in alphabetical order. After all her expensive education, she was reduced to doing her own filing. What a waste.

The image of the hospital room continued to flicker behind her eyes. It had been a mistake to visit there so late in the day. Erika hated hospitals, and unpleasant memories of them began to surface. She shook her head to clear her mind of everything but the task in front of her.

Thirty minutes later, a noise from the hall caught her attention. She raised her head to see Alice Miller leaning on the office door. Alice laughed quietly, an edge of caution in her tone. "How was your day?"

"I've had better," Erika answered with equal caution.

"Did I ruin it?"

Erika tried to smile and failed. "You'd better believe it. You really trounced me in the hearing this morning. You show no mercy. How could you?"

Alice shifted her weight and crossed her ankles. "It was easy. You deserved it—coming before a judge with such shabby evidence. The charges against my client should have been dropped."

Red flooded into Erika's face. "I know you're right, but you know how I hate to lose."

Alice tilted her head. "Even to your best friend?"

"Even to my best friend," Erika admitted, waving her hand toward a chair. "Sit down. I want to ask you something about this morning."

Alice eased down in the chair. "Don't ask. We both know the boy was guilty, but my duty as a public defender is to provide my client with the best possible defense." She smiled and looked directly at Erika. "Meaning, I must see to it no one steps on my client's rights, including you. And don't pout, Ms. Assistant DA, you'll have your chance to zap me one of these days, and I doubt I'll take it any better than you."

Ordinarily, the prospect of zapping Alice would have restored her spirits, but today was an exception. It was going to take more. Erika managed a weak grin. "Thank God we're friends, Alice. You're a formidable adversary in court, and I'd hate to have you for an enemy."

"Right you are," Alice agreed, her tone adding a touch of salt to the wound. "But from the looks of you, I don't think I'm your only problem today. What's up?"

"Juvenile division," Erika snapped. "Perhaps moving here was a mistake."

Alice patted her hand. "I wondered at the time if it was a wise move for you. If I were you, I'd avoid juvenile like the plague. After Rick, it must be difficult."

"What choice did I have? With the DA's policy to rotate all of his assistants to all departments, I'd have had to tell him the sordid saga of my brother, and even then, there was no guarantee he would have excused me." Erika rose and paced around the room slowly, eyeing the decor critically. "I admit being here reminds me constantly of Rick, but I think about him every day anyway. It's just . . ." She began to twist her hair. "Well, it seems every kid in Denver has gone bad."

Alice turned, and her brown eyes followed Erika. "Just like Rick?"

"In a way."

"What Rick did to you was wrong, not to mention in . . ."

Erika's pensive voice interrupted her. "Rick's been gone almost two years. I don't know why he ran away without a word. If I'd known what was wrong, maybe I could've stopped him." She paused and looked at a dreary seascape hanging on the wall. "Last month was his eighteenth birthday." She faced Alice stiffly. "You never understood. The money he took from me didn't matter."

"Let's not argue through it again, Erika. We'll never agree about Rick. And stop fiddling with your hair, you'll ruin it."

Erika dropped her hand, responding to Alice's order. Her pacing slowed even more. "Okay, enough of Rick." She made a small face at the walls of the room. "I didn't realize how unprepared I was for the gravity of crimes committed by kids, but today enlightened me. I questioned an arsonist, a rapist, four junior high students who operated a drug ring, and I just returned from the hospital where a woman is dying. She won't regain consciousness because of a beating her husband gave her before their fourteen-year-old daughter stabbed him to death. Can you imagine that? What's unbelievable is I may have to prosecute all of them." She felt the sting of tears and reached for a tissue from a box atop her desk as she passed. Returning, she sat down. "I'm not sure I can do that. Could you?" She dabbed at her eyes with determination, managing to control the tears.

Alice answered her question bluntly. "I could if they're guilty. Are they?"

"All except the girl who killed her father attempting to save her mother's life. Well, she killed him, but she won't be charged with murder." Erika stopped short, then sighed. "The girl's father is dead and her mother is dying. What'll she do?"

"If I know you, Erika, you'll find some way to help her." Impatience crept into Alice's voice. "Please stop fretting over your day. You can't change it now."

Erika eyed her friend. "You won't let me feel sorry for myself, will you?"

"Sure I will, but enough is enough." Alice made an outrageous face. Alice was tall, thin, dark and extremely graceful, like a model on the cover of a high-fashion magazine. Her ability to completely destroy her sultry beauty always shocked Erika and made her laugh. A little chuckle escaped Alice as her face moulded itself into another ridiculous contortion. Both women eased into a tumult of cleansing laughter.

"You win! I've had it with being down. It's nonproductive." Erika wiped her eyes. "Time to change the subject. Do you have a date for Saturday night?"

"I do. You know Ted Parsons." Alice's manner indicated more than pleasure with her answer. Erika thought she looked downright smug.

Alice always seemed to snag the good ones, and it was difficult for Erika not to show her envy. "I admire your choice," she remarked a bit too coolly. "You'll make a handsome couple." Inwardly bracing for the objection which was bound to come, Erika watched warily as she said, "Josh is taking me." Alice's eyes narrowed in disappointment. "Don't do that," Erika ordered, "Josh is just a friend."

Alice shrugged. "That's what you keep telling me, but it doesn't alter the fact Josh is the police department's resident Lothario, and he's forty if he's a day. That's much too old for you, and besides, you can do better than Josh Manning."

"His romantic reputation is highly overrated." Alice's eyes questioned her remark. "It is. What do I have to do to convince you Josh and I are friends and that's all."

Alice's hands indicated surrender. "I suppose I shouldn't be too critical of Josh. He *is* trying to help you locate Rick."

Pleased that her friend conceded one point, Erika flashed her prettiest smile. "I'm looking forward to the party. It's kind of the Denver Bar Association to provide a special diversion during this long, hot summer. Dinner and dancing in an elegant atmosphere appeals to me. I have no objection to a taste of the good life."

Alice started for the door. "Me either." She glanced at her watch. "It's almost quitting time. Come have a drink with me."

"Can't. These papers must be filed before I go home and change. I'm meeting Josh for an early dinner this evening."

Alice waltzed out of the room without looking back. "Talk to you tomorrow," she called.

Later, Erika found time had closed in on her. In a rush, she carried her briefcase to the hall and returned to her desk, scooping the things she wanted to take home with her into her arms. As she slipped the key into the lock of her office door, everything she held began to slip from her grasp. A voice from behind startled her, and all of the things fell to the floor, scattering about the hall.

She wheeled around to see a man bending to retrieve her belongings. His masculine voice was deep and clear, his statement bordered on an order. "Let me get them." He picked up a folder, tucked the papers back inside and placed it under his arm. His strong fingers gripped her cassette recorder as he held it to his ear and shook it gently. "At least it doesn't rattle. I doubt it's broken." With his left hand, he retrieved the last item, a book, and glanced at the title. "*Contract Law*? Can't an attractive young lady find something more interesting to read?"

She heard the sound of her own breath as she sucked it in, too astonished at his appearance to take notice of his remark. The noticeably expensive suit was tailored to accentuate wide shoulders, slender waist and hips. He returned her things to her outstretched hands and smiled. "My fault entirely. Sorry I startled you." One hand raked the full, dark hair from his face as deep brown eyes surveyed her slender body. A twinkle in them told her he approved of what he saw. His open appraisal embarrassed her, but she couldn't imagine why; she was appraising him in the same manner. She felt a warm flush rising to her face, and lost the staring contest. She looked down, hating the redness creeping upward. It would expose her vulnerability. She forced a calm tone. "Thanks for helping me."

He placed his hands on his hips in an arrogant stance. "It's the least I can do since it's my error. I had no intention of slipping up on you. You must have been busy with your thoughts." He made no move to leave. What did he want, an apology? I didn't ask for his help, she thought. He indicated her briefcase with a nod. "Is that yours?" Erika bobbed her head. His tone was either condescending or impatient. It was condescending, she decided. He lifted the case and held it flat before her. "If you'd put all your junk in here, you might avoid another accident." With one efficient motion, he snapped open the latches with his thumbs and waited.

Her pride smarted and her blue eyes flashed. She hurriedly dumped everything into the case with a solid thud and snapped it closed with a flourish. It was obvious that he thought her nothing but a flighty female, and once more, her cheeks colored. She hoped her effort to regain her composure wasn't evident. "You've been very kind. Thank you." She turned to leave, eager to end this uncomfortable interview.

"Don't forget these," she heard him say. Glancing over her shoulder, she saw him draw the keys to her office from the door. He dangled them between his fingers, an amused smile on his face. His eyes danced at her dilemma.

No longer able to disguise her irritation, she strode the distance between them, took the keys from his hand and spit out the word "Thanks," then hurried down the hall. What now, she thought angrily as he called to her again.

"Miss, can you tell me where I might find the district attorney's office? I know he moved recently and I'm afraid I'm lost. My name is Mitch Logan and I have an appointment with him."

His casual manner didn't keep her heart from jumping or her

stomach from sinking when she recognized the famous name. Yet she managed to pull herself together and point down the hall. "Go to the corner. Mr. Renquist's office is the third door on the right." She smiled to herself because she sounded unimpressed with his famous name.

Mitch Logan tipped an imaginary hat and bowed slightly. "Thank you, my dear. It's been a pleasure meeting you."

Erika was impressed as she watched him swagger around the corner. How could she help it? Logan was the most sought-after defense lawyer in the Rocky Mountains. His name struck fear in the heart of every prosecuting attorney from California to Colorado. She tilted her head and really smiled for the first time since they met. No wonder he seldom lost a case. His presence and attitude during their brief encounter reduced her to a wriggling, speechless female: a long-forgotten feeling. Think what he could do to a jury. She walked through the halls of the Denver City and County Building forgetting her miserable day. He was younger, and definitely better-looking, than his pictures. What a lawyer, she thought and sighed with envy.

Erika stepped outside into the glaring Colorado sunlight. The heat from the cement sidewalk struck her like a blow. Denver was hot in July. One quick glance in both directions and she darted across the street to the parking lot. If she hurried she would only be fashionably late for her date.

As she parked the car near the restaurant, she spied Josh waiting in the courtyard. Alice was probably right about his being too old for her, but this was hardly a romance, after all. The difference in their ages might account for the fact that the relationship was strictly platonic, though when they'd first met he had made a few amorous noises. Erika had the impression that had been more from habit than true interest, and since she hadn't been interested either, they settled into a comfortable friendship. He was still courtly toward her, in an old-fashioned way she enjoyed.

She hurried to meet him. He was rather good-looking, she

supposed, in a nondescript way: medium height, slightly chunky build with a round, friendly face. Too bad there just weren't any sparks. "How's my favorite detective?" she asked, offering him both her hands.

A grin lit his tanned face. "Fine. I've been waiting impatiently for my favorite lawyer." He took her hands and kissed her forehead. "You look lovely, Erika. I like your dress. It matches your eyes and you look cool, even on a night as hot as this." Josh never missed a chance to compliment her. She appreciated that and she smiled at him warmly. Josh always reminded her she was every inch a female. Perhaps that was the secret of his romantic reputation.

A waiter greeted them immediately after the hostess seated them at a secluded table covered with a red checkered tablecloth. A Chianti bottle with a crooked burning candle sat glumly between them. Only the excellent Italian food kept customers returning here, not the decor. Erika anticipated Josh's remark. "It's not the Ritz," they said in unison, then laughed. The waiter offered a menu, but Josh shook his head and looked at her. "The usual?"

"The usual," she answered. Josh ordered Chianti, spaghetti with sausage, green salad and garlic bread. "We'll have coffee and spumoni later." The waiter left and he asked, "Do you get the feeling we're in a rut?"

Erika's manner was languid. "I don't mind the rut. It's a pleasant one, and no place in Denver serves better Italian food."

As the evening progressed, they ate and drank, talking easily, completely comfortable with each other. When the dessert and coffee arrived and the waiter retired, Erika pushed her ice cream away and reached for the coffee. "I can't eat another bite. The dinner was delicious as usual, and I stuffed myself again. Thanks for asking me."

A hint of concern flickered in his eyes. You won't thank me when I tell you I can't go to the DBA dance with you Saturday."

She brought her head up sharply. "Why?"

"I'm leaving tonight at eleven for Detroit to pick up a prisoner. I won't be back in time. With vacations and all, we're short-handed downtown, and I drew the duty. I would've told you earlier, but I just found out this afternoon. I'm sorry, Erika."

Regret was evident in her voice. "I'm sorry too." She fingered the handle of her cup. "I was looking forward to the party." She stopped and sipped her coffee.

"Find someone else to take you. A beautiful, enterprising young woman like you shouldn't have any trouble."

It was really too late to start looking, and Erika knew it. "I'll try," she said unconvincingly.

Josh reached for her hand and held it. "I know I've let you down. What can I do to make it up to you?"

She wrinkled her nose at him. "Call me after you get back. We'll try to think of something."

He squeezed her hand before letting go and leaned back in his chair. "I ruined your day, didn't I?"

"It was pretty much a loss before I got here. I don't know if juvenile division and I are going to make it."

"Rick didn't help you there, did he?"

"You're the second person today to tell me that. It must be true, but I don't think all the things Rick did had that much influence. He was only fifteen when our parents died, and we stayed together for almost a year before he ran away. You know living with me wouldn't be easy."

"It wasn't easy for either of you."

"I didn't mind. Really, I didn't." Her hand went to her hair and she straightened it instead of twisting it. "He's my only living relative." A chilling thought grew in the back of her mind. She shivered. Rick may be dead.

Josh's face darkened. "Taking your money was bad enough, but he took more. I'd bet the notions you had of being able to solve every problem and being entirely independent are dented some?"

Green and blue eyes met; the blue ones blazed for only a moment. "You're right, but I'm healing, and I still like to make it on my own."

"Erika, no one makes it on their own. Everyone needs help."

Erika's sigh signaled dissatisfaction with his remark. "An old family trait, I guess. My parents made it through the Depression working hard and never accepting help. As long as my father lived, he couldn't forgive Roosevelt for all those assistance programs. He used to say that too much help from others weakens the recipient."

"But your folks were paying your way through law school. You didn't work before they died."

"I did in the summers," she countered. "No one loafed at our house. The folks felt obligated to support Rick and me until we finished our formal education. They also believed our grades were important. We were expected to concentrate on the job of getting an education. A's and B's were the only acceptable grades."

"Did Rick do well in school?"

"You know he did. You checked his school records."

Josh looked surprised. "I don't remember telling you about that."

"You didn't," Erika said flatly.

Josh restated the position she had heard from him before. "Paying back the money Rick took from the garage where he worked was a mistake, Erika. If he was wanted for a felony, the police would be actively looking for him. As it is, they do very little to find runaways."

Her eyes clouded. No one but Josh knew Rick had stolen money from the garage where he worked. She was too ashamed to tell anyone else. "And I'll tell you again, I paid back the money he stole from the garage because I didn't want Rick saddled with a criminal charge then, and I don't want it now. He was young, and I can't think of him as a criminal. He simply wasn't that way. You didn't know him, Josh. Rick wasn't a bad kid."

12

Josh moved in his chair uneasily. "How much did it cost you to keep believing Rick was a good kid?"

Her eyes sparked. "That's not fair!"

"Nothing's fair. How much, Erika?"

"A little over four thousand dollars." Her shoulders fell and the anger was gone. "That includes the money he took from our apartment, the garage, and the bills he left."

The corner of Josh's mouth quivered. "That much," he managed to say.

"Our inheritance wasn't large, especially since it was divided equally between us. I received my share immediately, and was able to continue school, but Rick wasn't twenty-one. He can't claim his money until then. Apparently, my parents believed twenty-one was the magical age for financial maturity." She sounded flippant and felt ashamed. "I'm the older, so I'm responsible for him. And I've failed miserably."

"It's none of my business, but what happens to the money if Rick doesn't return?"

She frowned and shrugged. "The money sits there gaining interest. I can't touch it unless he dies without heirs before he's twenty-one."

"That seems a bit harsh. Unfair to you, I mean."

"What gave you that idea?" she snapped. "It's fair. I don't want his money. I only want to know he's alive and well."

Josh looked thoughtful and rapped his knuckles on the table. "I'll keep trying to find him. He's been gone long enough to get brave and apply for a driver's license or something of the sort. When he does, his prints will give him away. Your brother is not your average runaway." His smile was designed to restore her confidence. "He's smart like his older sister." The waiter arrived with the check. Josh paid him, then held her chair as she stood. "We'll find him, Erika, I promise."

Her lips touched his cheek. "It helps to know someone is trying, and I can't thank you enough for your efforts."

Erika drove home speculating on her life. Fate had spared her most disappointments until her parents died, and then Rick walked out on her, crushing her ideas of family and honesty. After two years she was still unable to accept what he had done. What happened to him to make him do such awful things? His stealing and running away were out of character.

Before reaching her apartment, she shook off the thoughts of her brother and concentrated on the events of the day, putting them in their proper perspective. Dropping that, she planned for the future. As long as she could remember, she had wanted to be a famous defense attorney. After graduating from law school, she chose the DA's office because she was offered a job, and it gave her an opportunity to see how the other half lived before she struck out on her own. The experience of thinking and working like a prosecutor was bound to help. Now, all she needed was money to finance her private practice. She had a plan, and she had to stick to it. Erika had never questioned her choice until yesterday, when she was transferred to juvenile. Today, her doubts were magnified.

# Chapter Two

THE MORNING WAS busy, but satisfying. Erika decided to skip lunch and relax with a cup of coffee. In an hour and ten minutes, she had to be in court and, afterwards, attend a conference with a girl who had broken parole. The girl's parents would be with her and the meeting promised to be an emotional one. She looked forward to a few quiet moments alone so she could map out the rest of the day.

Barely settled down, she was confronted by Rhonda, the office secretary, who placed two slips of paper on her desk and said in a soft midwestern twang, "You're to return these calls, and Mr. Renquist just left the office." Erika saw her eyes glisten with excitement. "His wife's gone to the hospital. Their new baby is on its way. Isn't that neat?" She rambled on, not waiting for an answer. "He won't be back today and he asked if you'd handle this for him." She handed Erika a blue folder.

"What is it?"

"A record of traffic offenses accumulated by some guy. Mr. Renquist was to meet with his lawyer at four-thirty today. Another plea-bargaining session, I presume."

Erika expressed her relief with a sigh. "I'm glad it isn't anything major. I have enough to handle today, and I'd like to get home early. Today's Friday."

"Wouldn't everyone," Rhonda replied and stalked from the room. She's sulking, Erika thought. I didn't *oooh* and *aaah* and visit over the new baby. She smiled inwardly. I'll have to do it next time and make her happy. Erika heard voices outside, and Rhonda returned immediately carrying flowers covered with green tissue. "This should brighten your day," she said, holding the flowers above her head. "No one, absolutely no one, has ever gotten flowers since I've been here. Flowers are so romantic. How did you get so lucky?"

Surprised, Erika caught her breath. "Are those for me?" Rhonda nodded and Erika walked around the desk and took them from her. She removed the covering and saw tiny rose buds: red and yellow ones, mixed with white baby's breath and greenery. Impressed with their delicate beauty, she whispered, "Aren't they lovely?"

Rhonda was openly curious. "I know. They're beautiful, but I want to know who they're from."

"I have no idea who sent them," Erika answered before she began to giggle. Caught up in Rhonda's eagerness, she fumbled for the card and had trouble getting it out of the small envelope. She read it and sighed with disappointment. "There's no signature. I don't know who sent them. Look!" She shoved the card at Rhonda, who promptly looked on the back. Finding nothing, she read the message on the front.

"By any chance are you free Saturday evening?" Rhonda looked at Erika. "Well, are you?"

"Am I what?"

"Free, Saturday?"

Erika caressed one of the rosebuds, feeling its rich softness. "Yes, as a matter of fact, I am."

Rhonda wrung her hands. "This is terrible. Someone wants a date with you and you don't know who it is."

Rhonda hit very close to home. In a way, it was terrible. Men were not as available as they once were. Refusing invitations during her last year in college because of classes, work, and studying resulted in fewer invitations from eligible men, and finally most stopped calling completely. Erika couldn't blame them for giving up on her; she was seldom available. Here at work, the men were either married or only interested in casual sex. Neither situation appealed to her. It was a sorry plight for an attractive woman who would turn twenty-six in October, one she would have to remedy when her career was firmly established.

Erika flushed, certain Rhonda was reading her thoughts. "It's a shame," she said, "but maybe the florist can tell us who sent the flowers. Date or no date, I should thank my admirer, whoever he is."

"Why didn't I think of that?" Rhonda opened the bottom drawer of the desk and found the phone book. "I can't stand a mystery, so I'm going to call right now." She leafed through the large book beaming with delight, but before she could find the number, the phone rang. After answering, she raised her eyebrows and covered the receiver with her hand. "It's Ted Parsons. He called you earlier." She bent her head in the direction of the messages on the desk. "He's the new dreamboat in the public defender's office. Could he have sent the flowers?"

Erika shook her head. "I'll call the florist later. And I promise I'll let you know who sent the flowers, as soon as I know." Rhonda was out of her office when she raised the phone and said, "Erika Wheatly."

"Ted Parsons. How are you this morning, Erika?"

His familiarity startled her, since she'd never met him. "I'm fine," she answered with caution.

"Alice has told me so much about you, I feel I already know you." There was a slight pause before he continued. "I'm assigned to the Maria Sanchez case. You know, the girl who stabbed her father. Is there a chance we could get together and talk about her today?"

Erika hesitated. She was certain her afternoon was full, but she checked anyway. "I'm looking at my schedule," she explained. She wanted to talk to him about the Sanchez girl and she didn't want to lose the opportunity. "I have a meeting at four-thirty. Could we do it after that?"

He said, "Oh," and fell silent. She began to wonder if he'd left the phone when he asked, "Have you had lunch?"

"No."

"I'm downstairs in the lobby waiting for Alice. Why don't

17

you eat with us, and we can talk about Maria and save a bit of time.''

Erika liked his thinking, and getting home early today still appealed to her. Also, she could use this chance to explain to Alice why she wouldn't be at the dinner dance tomorrow. She rushed to answer. "No problem. I'll be right there."

After lunch, Erika hurried to court, then rushed to her conference. Pressed for time, she didn't return to her office until minutes before her meeting for Renquist. She sat down to read the traffic record of Martin May, shaking her head at the long list of violations. This young man and his lawyer would have a hard time getting any concessions from her. His record was an appalling account of immaturity. It was all too apparent that May was a danger to the total population when he was behind the wheel. A touch of weariness caught her as she picked up the folder and went to Renquist's office for her last official duty of the day.

At ten to five, she prepared to leave when Mitch Logan entered the office. Again, impeccably dressed and feloniously handsome. Looking at him caused her to wonder how she could have put him out of her mind. She hoped fervently that today would offer the chance to make a better impression. In a clear cool tone, she said, "Please sit down, Mr. Logan. I've been waiting for you. For quite a while," she couldn't resist adding.

She saw a crooked smile appear. "I'd have been more prompt if I'd known you were waiting, but unfortunately my appointment is with Dick Renquist."

She sat down and clarified the circumstances. "Mr. Renquist's second child chose to be born today. He's at the hospital with his wife. He asked me to make his apologies and meet with you." She offered her hand. "I'm Erika . . ."

He took her hand and held it. "You're Erika Wheatly," he said. "After our interesting meeting last evening, I asked Dick about you."

There was an awkward pause. It was almost as if he expected her to say something, but what? A small frown wrinkled her face as the silence continued. He let go of her hand and sat down across from her, looking somewhat uncomfortable. Their eyes met, and unspoken questions from each collided. Erika noted, now that she faced him calmly, that he was not exactly handsome, or as Rhonda would say, a dreamboat. Instead, he was rugged looking, projecting strength, magnetism and self-confidence to an inordinate degree. Maybe overly confident and vain. Yes, definitely vain. She was also certain he knew others were drawn to him and that he used this attraction to his advantage.

He broke the silence somewhat grudgingly. "I apologize for being late. I won't waste any more of your time. My client, Martin May, has a traffic record unequaled by anyone. He'll be arraigned Monday afternoon. As far as the recent reckless driving charge is concerned, we'll plead guilty and gladly pay the fine, but with his record, I anticipate much more than a fine. Martin has a job at night and attends summer school because he failed his last semester in high school. Our problem is not the fine. It's dealing with the punishment that's bound to be levied."

They settled down to a nuts-and-bolts bargaining session, agreeing quickly on a satisfactory solution. Erika rather enjoyed it, since she held all the cards. Mitch Logan was apparently doing a favor for a friend, the father of this menace at the wheel.

Erika finished her notes and looked at Mitch. "I'll do my best to convince the judge to allow Martin to do his detention on weekends so he can stay in school. You see to it that he stays away from driving." She looked at her watch. They had nothing left to discuss, but he seemed reluctant to leave. "Why didn't you call about this, Mr. Logan? You'd have achieved the same results and saved a trip."

He sounded as if what he was saying was the last thing in the world on his mind. "When I ask a favor of someone, the least I can do is to make my request in person. Even if it's a small request." His deep brown eyes questioned her again.

Erika squirmed. What is he after? What does he want from me? She tugged at her hair. Resolving that today was not going to be the disaster of yesterday, she met the awkward moment head-on. "You want something. What is it?"

"I expected a call from you today." He looked away to avoid her gaze. "At least, I hoped you'd call."

"And why would I call you?" Her voice trailed into nothing as she saw him bristle, his eyes riveted to hers.

"To thank me for the flowers, and to answer my question."

"My God, the flowers! You sent them?" He nodded. The heat of embarrassment flooded through her. She started to apologize, but decide to forgo it for now. "Follow me, Mr. Logan. I want you to see something." Walking to her office, she was very aware of his nearness. She felt the heat from his body and smelled his spicy scent. Mitch Logan was an appealing man, even if he knew he was. In her office, she found the unsigned card and handed it to him. Erika watched him closely while he examined it. "As you see, the card is not signed. I didn't know who sent the flowers. I was going to call the florist, but today was busy and I completely forgot until you mentioned them." Once more, her voice failed as she ended the sentence. She cleared her throat. "They're beautiful, Mr. Logan. Thank you."

He stood looking at her, seemingly ignoring what she was saying. "You haven't answered my question."

"I'm free tomorrow night. What did you have in mind?" She hated the slight quiver in her voice.

His small crooked smile reappeared. "How does the DBA dinner dance at the Hilton sound?"

Her heart pounded. "Wonderful."

"Good. I'll call for you at seven, if that's satisfactory?"

Erika reached for a pencil on her desk. "Fine. Let me write down my address for you." His hand stopped hers, the touch sent a tingle darting up her arm.

"Never mind. I know where you live." Once more she was nonplussed, and she gaped at him. "I'm looking forward to tomorrow night, Erika, and please call me Mitch.'' He winked and waved goodbye.

"Mitch it is,'' she stammered as she heard the sound of his footsteps echoing down the hall. So that's what he wanted, a date with her. "I can't believe it,'' she cried when she was sure he could no longer hear. She whirled around and dropped in a chair. All manner of thoughts crowded her mind. Why me? Oh, me and the great Mitch Logan. The excitement of the invitation gripped her and the anticipation started to grow. She sat stunned and thrilled for a few more minutes until self-impatience drove her to gather her homework for the weekend. This time she packed each item neatly in her briefcase, left the office, then returned quickly to get the flowers.

A blaring horn jolted her from her continued reverie before she had driven two blocks. Appalled at her state of mind, she directed her attention to driving. There was a lot to do. Tonight she would make the plans.

Satisfied with her Saturday morning shopping trip, Erika unpacked groceries and stored them away. She crossed shopping from the list made Friday night. Next, in the bedroom, she selected and arranged her clothes for the following week, making sure they didn't need pressing or repair and then hanging them, in order, in her neat closet. The second item on her list was now complete.

The state of being organized pleased her, and she hummed while she changed her clothes and smoothed the front of her flowered wraparound skirt and tightened the belt. It matched the bikini underneath and provided a modest cover for her short walk to the pool. Stopping at the hall closet, she found a towel and suntan lotion, then hurried to meet Alice. She was eager to see the look on her friend's face when she told her about her date tonight.

Erika shaded her eyes from the shock of the sun, looked around the pool and spied Alice's lithe body stretched on a lawn chair. "Sorry I'm late,'' she said as she approached, "but I'm organized for next week. Now I'm free to do as I please.''

Alice raised her head and sunglasses to look at her. "You rat, you wore a bikini."

Erika finished removing her skirt and sat down next to her. "That's all I have."

"That figures. Only people with shapes like yours take them for granted."

Alice could wear anything she chose. Why a bikini spooked her was a mystery to Erika. "It's lack of nerve, not lack of figure. You'd find out if you ever tried one."

Alice lay back shaking her head. "No. I'm too long. I look like a pole with two ribbons tied to it." She sighed loudly, "But on you, a bikini looks good."

Erika began applying lotion on her arms and shoulders. She didn't want to talk about bikinis, she wanted to talk about Mitch Logan. She wracked her brain for a way to introduce the subject, applying lotion to her legs, then adjusting her chair to lie flat. Alice seemed quite content to stay there without talking. Unable to contain her news any longer, Erika raised herself up on her elbow, watching Alice closely. "Guess I'll be seeing you at the party tonight after all, I have a date."

Alice didn't move. "I can tell by your voice you can't wait to tell me, so who is it?"

Erika watched closely. "Would you believe Mitchell Logan?"

Her friend bolted upright, to Erika's satisfaction. "You're joking. You can't mean it?"

Erika's eyes gleamed as she laughed, raising her right hand in a solemn vow. "I do. Scout's honor."

"How?" Alice shouted. Her loudness prompted her to look around to see if anyone near was watching. Erika launched into the story of her two encounters with Mitch, attempting to remember every word and gesture that passed between them. When she finished, Alice shook her head and muttered, "If it were anyone but you, I wouldn't believe it."

"It better be true, or I've gone to a lot of trouble. My clothes are ready, I went to the safety deposit box to get my mother's diamond earrings and necklace, and . . . ." She stopped to grin slyly. "And I looked up Logan at the library." Suddenly Erika felt impelled to justify spying on Mitch. "Well, he questioned Dick Renquist about me, so I decided it was only fair I know something about him." She ended with a toss of her head to indicate she was proud of her detective work.

"I love it!" Alice rubbed her hands together in wanton expectation. "What did we find out?" Although she tried to suppress a squeal, part of it found its way to the surface.

Erika attempted to be grave. "For one thing, his reputation as a lawyer is solid as a rock, but we already knew that." She wrinkled her nose and half-shrugged. "Apparently, he's rich. He owns and flies a plane, and he does a great deal of charity work, but what I like best is there's no mention of wife or children."

"How old is he?"

"The book said thirty-five, but he looks thirty, and I'm here to testify he's better looking than his pictures. Better looking in a rugged sort of way." She paused and took a breath. She had a tendency to hurry when excited. "He wasn't as tall as I expected." Raising her hand above her head she studied it a second. "Considering my heels, I suspect he's not over five-ten. Maybe even shorter. I don't know. Who cares?"

A slow groan slipped from Alice. "You mean he has sex appeal. How can you sit here and talk so calmly about a date with Mitchell Logan? I get goose pimples just thinking about it." Alice shifted her body to face Erika. "If you don't introduce me to him tonight, our friendship is off, finished, kaput."

"Alice, he's just a man."

"You're kidding."

"Of course, but it sounded good," Erika quipped.

"Sometimes I don't know about you. You're independent and not easily impressed. You're the only woman I know who wouldn't flip over that man."

Erika dropped her head. "Oh, I could flip all right, but it's only a date. One date doesn't mean much."

"Huh! You don't have to date a man to know you like him.

The first time I saw Ted, I knew I would marry him if he'd ask me. I didn't expect it to happen to me, but it did. How did you feel the first time you saw Mitch?''

''So it's Mitch now,'' Erika teased. Alice glared and she rushed the rest of her words. ''Shock at his magnetism, anger, embarrassment, but certainly not love. You surprise me, Alice. No one believes in love at first sight.''

Alice covered a yawn with her hand. ''When it happens, it happens. I'll be Mrs. Ted Parsons if I have anything to say about it. I just hope it won't interfere with my career.'' She stifled another yawn. ''I envy you, Erika. You plan your life and take it step by step. I wish I were more like you. I float with the tide and take my chances.''

For the first time, Erika felt uneasy. Certainly, she was a careful planner, of her time and of her life. But if Alice had the impression that she had it all under control, she was mistaken. Turmoil over the death of her parents and Rick running away nagged at her constantly. Inside, she fought against every unpleasant event that happened to her. That's why she felt she must be organized, she needed some control over her life. Erika stood and walked to the edge of the pool. ''I'm going in. Join me?''

Alice scarcely moved. ''You can't swim in a bikini,'' she drawled.

''Who said swim? I'm just going to cool off for a while.''

With amazing speed, Alice jumped up and ran for the pool, diving in with expertise and grace. When she surfaced, she teased, ''Try that in your bikini.''

Later in the afternoon, when Alice left, she hugged Erika and said, ''I want to meet Mitch tonight and judge for myself if he's good enough for my best friend.''

At almost seven, the hour of reckoning was at hand. Erika found it hard to smile. After Alice left, she kept busy cleaning the apartment and getting ready, but now it was impossible to think of anything but Mitch Logan. Leaving her chair, she went to the mirror near the door and looked at her reflection. Slightly better than average, she thought. She glanced around the room for the third time. It was gleaming, and the roses added a pleasant fragrance to the air. They were displayed on the table near the door where they couldn't be missed.

Her body jerked at the sound of the doorbell. He was on time. Her hand shook as she reached for the door. She stiffened her spine, reminding herself this wasn't her first date and she should stop acting as if it were. Forcing a smile, she opened the door. "Hi," she said, hearing it come out limp and quiet. Her planned greeting couldn't make it through her paralyzed throat, a phenomenon which happened each time she saw him. Mitch leaned on the door frame waiting. "Hi," he answered.

He looked different in formal clothes. He seemed taller and less broad, more hard-muscled and lean. Had she forgotten this or just hadn't noticed before? Pausing to glance at him did nothing to restore her confidence, or to improve her tight throat. She stepped aside and murmured, "Come in."

In one move, he was inside and taking both of her hands. It was impossible not to be held by his gleaming eyes. "You look stunning, lady. In fact, you're beautiful." Somewhat awkwardly, since she was too astounded to help him, he bent to kiss her cheek. The kiss was just a peck, ritually performed, and the thrill she expected wasn't there.

"Would you like a drink before we go?" she asked. The slight disappointment she felt urged her to hope he would decline the invitation. She withdrew her hands from his reluctantly.

"I'd like one. What do you have?" He rubbed his hands together giving the impression he was warming them, and followed her to the kitchen. "Bourbon and water is my favorite, but if you don't have it, it's no big deal."

"That I can do," she answered. In the kitchen, she realized for the first time how small it was. With him there, space was at a premium. She found the whiskey and took the ice from the fridge. Without looking his way, she knew he was appraising the apartment and her.

"That's a lovely dress," he remarked casually. "I like long dresses." He reached out quickly to catch the ice tray slipping from her hands and placed it on the counter. "Do you wear pink often?"

Her back was turned so he couldn't see her roll her eyes. "No. Why?"

"Don't get me wrong, I like the color, and you look very nice in it, but I'd bet you dinner at the Quorum there won't be another pink dress at the party tonight. Women seem to be dressing in beige, blue, and white during the summer. It's refreshing to know you dare to be different."

Erika licked her lips. She knew something he didn't know. "Any pink dress, counselor?"

"Any," he answered with confidence.

"If I held you to your bet, you'd lose."

"No. I'll win. It gives me an excuse to watch the ladies, and if anyone else wears the color, I get to take you out again. Either way, I win."

She could barely contain her laughter. Even though she tried, a chuckle slipped out. "I'm positive I'll win. A dinner at the Quorum is quite expensive just for an excuse to ogle females when you'll do it anyway."

"I made the bet. I'll stick with it. Anyway a small wager adds spice to the evening."

Erika pondered his idea of a small wager. If she lost, the Quorum would destroy her budget. "And I'll take the bet, but only if it's a Coke, fries, and a Big Mac at McDonald's."

"You're on," he said, sounding satisfied. He turned and stood looking toward the living room.

Erika didn't have the heart to tell him that the last time she was at the Hilton the waitresses wore pink uniforms. Serves him right, she thought. Anticipating his expression, when he discovered what she already knew, amused her, and she hurried to finish making the drinks.

"You have a nice place, and I imagine it's practical for you. It would be difficult for you to work and keep a large place at the same time."

"I could manage a larger place, but I don't see any point in having a bigger apartment. This one is fine." She almost ran into him when she turned to hand him his drink. Their touching fingers made her arm tingle. "You aren't one of those men who believe a woman can't work and manage a household at the same time, are you?"

He appeared surprised at her remark. "Not I. I admire women. It's unbelievable what they can do. No one can handle as many divorce cases as I have and not discover how clever women are."

She walked by him carefully after pouring herself a glass of white wine. His last statement didn't set well. She settled on the divan, indicating with her hand for him to join her. She decided he could have meant so many things that it would be safer ignoring his remark. Raising her glass slightly, Erika offered a toast. "Here's to lawyers who understand women."

"Touché," he said restraining his laughter. They both sipped their drinks and he settled forward, holding his drink in both hands. "I'll choose my words more carefully next time."

Erika regarded him. "Say what you mean or I'll never know how you really feel."

"See, I told you women are clever. You have placed me in the position of being absolutely truthful. Do you realize how devastating that can be for a man?"

"Or a woman," she snapped, pressing her lips together, but then sighed. "I'm sorry. I came on too strong." She lowered her eyes and watched her hands for a moment. "I have a problem talking to the living legend, Mitchell Logan. Does that happen to you often, or is it just me?"

"Is that a compliment?" he questioned. She nodded solemnly. He chuckled quietly. "It's happened to me before. In fact, it happens often, but you're the only one who admitted it. I think you're going to be good for me, Erika Wheatly. I need to be put in my place now and then. Intimidation is part of my role as a courtroom lawyer, and I'm afraid I tend to carry it over into my private life. It's a difficult habit to break." His eyes found hers. "You won't let me get away with it. You'll put me in my place when I need it."

She looked squarely at him over the edge of her wine glass. She set it down without drinking. "Will you take me to the party? I want to drink, eat, and dance the night away. I've looked forward to this event all summer, and I have a bet to win."

Mitch slapped his hands on his knees and stood. "That's what I like to hear. You and I like to do the same things."

In a matter of minutes, Erika was installed beside him in his Bronco. She relaxed and gave in to his charm. His brown eyes were intent on driving, his strong hands resting lightly on the steering wheel. His stunning profile and the muscles of his out-stretched leg moving beneath his black trousers worked to-gether to draw her under his spell. It relieved her to know he didn't intend to overwhelm her; yet, her natural wariness re-mained. He thought he intimidated her, and he did to some degree, but her quickness to blush, the increased warmth, and her unusual shyness weren't the result of coercion. Other people coerced her and she didn't react in this manner. She fussed with her dress. Just thinking about a special man in her life now made her uncomfortable. She had worked too hard too many years to get to this point in her life. Why should she complicate it? It was important for her to establish her career, then there would be time for romance.

Mitch asked, "What's going through your pretty head? You're deep in thought."

Caught, she stumbled over her words. "Oh, I'm just sur-prised at your car. I thought you would drive an Alfa Romeo or something European. I didn't expect a four-wheel drive." That was dumb, Erika, she told herself. You goofed. Quickly, she tried to cover her indiscretion. "It's new, isn't it?"

"Just bought it last week," he answered proudly.

Her eyes moved around the car and she breathed in. "A new car always has a certain smell that's pleasant."

He smiled. "I bought it because it's a mean machine." He thought for a moment. "It's just what I need, especially for the winter. My home's in Vail and I make a lot of trips up and down the hill. Even if I don't go home every day, some days I feel like an elevator, others like a yo-yo."

Erika heard a bit of regret in his voice. He was kidding, yet he wasn't. "What a long drive. You must spend a lot of time on the road, and what happens when you're stranded and have to stay in town?"

"I have an apartment here, but I seldom use it. My office is well-equipped and I usually stay there when I can't get home."

"That's handy," she mused thinking rather enviously that he had it all. A house in Vail, an apartment in town, and, as he phrased it, a well-equipped office. What was a very special evening on the town for her must seem commonplace to him.

29

# Chapter Three

THE SETTING INSIDE the spacious hall was one of cool sophistication, welcome on so warm a July evening. Mitch waved and smiled at friends as they found their assigned places at a table set for eight. They were the last of the eight to arrive, and Erika grew nervous as they approached. Making a small entrance was not what she wanted. After the introductions, Erika relaxed a bit. Ordinarily, she was not apprehensive when meeting new people, but tonight was different, and she didn't understand exactly why. Mitch's twinkling eyes and soothing charm gave her courage.

After sitting down she searched the room for a waitress. "Drat," she whispered faintly, as their friendly waitress appeared in a freshly starched white uniform. Erika glanced about once more and groaned. For the first time it occurred to her that special help was probably hired for banquets, explaining the white attire.

Dinner was delicious—crisp salad, steak, baked potato and a dessert she couldn't recognize, but it was light and fluffy, tasting of pineapple. During dinner, she located Alice and Ted at the far end of the room. Twice she looked in their direction and saw Alice's readable smile.

The dinner conversation convinced her Mitch was everything she wanted to be: articulate and smooth, established in a career, self-assured and well-liked. Erika became more an observer than a participant, watching a master at his craft. As the dialogue progressed, she questioned her moments of envy. With the tacit compliance of the others, Mitch fielded questions and changed the conversation to his liking. He manipulated all of them, and they permitted him to do so. He was the charming center of attention, and he loved it. Perhaps she envied him because he demanded attention and received it.

Erika found herself alone with Mitch when the band began to play in the adjoining room. They lingered over the last of their coffee. She laid her hand on his arm and spoke lazily, "I enjoyed the dinner. The food was delicious."

He tweaked her nose playfully. "I know. You didn't miss a bite of the entire meal. Do you always have a hearty appetite?"

"Almost always," she admitted frankly.

"Good. I can't abide picky eaters." He threw up his hands in a helpless gesture. "And I can't stand dieters. You wouldn't believe the number of people I know who are on diets."

She found it hard not to smile at his pompous outburst, but she couldn't resist the urge to needle him. "Be careful, you may have to eat your words one day."

He groaned and smirked. "That's a bad pun, Erika. A very bad pun."

"Yes it was," she laughed, "but enough talk about food." She rose and tugged at his arm. "I want you to meet my best friend first, then we'll dance."

He cooperated and let her pull him from the chair. He took her arm and walked behind her. As they wandered slowly around the tables, he bent slightly to hear her saying, "There they are."

"I hope your friend is the striking brunette in the corner. She's a real looker."

Erika smiled broadly, showing her beautiful teeth. "So's her date." She raised her hand and waved to Alice.

Mitch spoke softly and quickly. "You were so certain you'd win our bet. I thought you knew someone who might be wearing pink. Your friend isn't. I misjudged you. Sorry."

"The party's not over yet, counselor, and Alice isn't the only woman I know."

The introductions made, all of them walked towards the

music. Erika whispered to Alice, ''Tell me if you see anyone in a pink dress.''

Alice raised her eyebrows and nodded. ''Why?''

''Tell you later,'' Erika answered, taking Mitch's arm.

Only a few couples were dancing when they walked into the dimly lit room and stood waiting for their eyes to adjust. Two small bars, chairs, and tables edged the dance floor. Ted and Alice found a table as Mitch guided her directly onto the floor.

He drew her into his arms, and she stiffened at the touch of his body, resisting the surge of pleasure it caused. She felt his warmth and ventured a glance at his face when they began to move across the floor. His nearness excited her. ''You dance well, Erika. Finding a partner who knows how to follow is rare indeed in this age of rock and roll.''

She rested her head on his shoulder, giving in to his magnetic charm. ''I enjoy dancing, but I don't believe you have any trouble leading anyone. At the table tonight, we all danced to your tune.''

Mitch pushed her back and looked down at her. ''Did that bother you?''

She snuggled to him to avoid his eyes, but the feeling of his body caused a shudder at contact. ''Don't tell anyone. It might ruin my image, but it didn't bother me. I learned a lot from you. Anyway it's none of my business if people let you bully them. Just don't try it with me.''

He tightened his arm around her waist. She heard a low moan before he spoke. ''You're trouble, Erika, and that's a fact.''

Tight and snug in his arms, she didn't want to bandy words with him. She only wanted to relax and bask in the warmth she felt. His remark went unchallenged and they didn't talk again until the music stopped. At the bar, they picked up drinks and joined Ted and Alice at their table.

Sitting down was a mistake. Each time a conversation began, they were interrupted. It seemed everyone wanted to say hello or introduce someone to Mitch. The steady stream amused her for a while, but eventually she wanted him to herself. Yet, the parade was interesting to observe. Some came by simply to be seen with a prominent lawyer. Others wanted something from him and mentioned cases pending, but he brushed aside all business talk. Seeing for the first time an unpleasant side of fame, she felt sympathy for him and delight when a greeting was friendly and genuine.

A lull in the traffic finally came. Erika took his hand. "Dancing is safer," she said as he followed her to the floor.

He sighed a heavy sigh when they began to dance. "Now I remember why I haven't come to one of these affairs for the last three years."

Erika laughed and melted to him. "Why did you come this time? You must have known what would happen."

"I knew you wanted to come, so I reasoned you wouldn't refuse my invitation."

"How did you know I wanted to come to this party?"

"I just knew."

His answer only made her more curious. "Don't expect me to beg for an answer. Just tell me how you knew I wanted to come to this affair."

"Simple. I used an old lawyer trick. You put yourself in your client's shoes, then you understand him better. I ask myself what would a struggling assistant DA want to do. The answer was obvious."

"And if I'd said no, or had another date?"

"You didn't, and I'm happy about that." His arm squeezed her waist. Erika wished she hadn't pursued the subject. She didn't want to be thought of as a struggling anything.

Later Alice pointed out two more pink dresses. Granted they weren't the same shade as hers, but they were pink. Mitch accepted the loss gracefully, still insisting he had won the bet.

Returning from powdering their noses, Alice and Erika found their dates in an intense debate over a murder trial currently taking place in Kansas. Since the defendant and the victim once lived in Denver, the case made the papers regularly. As they sat down, Ted was saying, "I wouldn't use that defense. . . ."

The four of them settled happily into a prolonged and heated discussion of the fine points of the case. As the arguments progressed, Erika gradually found herself defending a position with which all the others, and particularly Mitch, totally disagreed. She stopped in mid-sentence, suddenly aware of her inner conflict. How could she oppose this man in anything? Yet, how could she not?

Erika's sudden silence gave Alice time to come to her aid. "Give up, friend of mine. You're outnumbered three to one." Alice's tone was light, and Erika was grateful for the opportunity her friend was giving her for a graceful retreat. She took a deep breath to collect herself. "Well," she said, "I won one bet today, so how about another wager, counselor? I believe Sara Bower will do time for the crime. Will a dinner at the Quorum be an enticing wager?"

Mitch deliberated a few seconds, and a deep frown brought his eyebrows together. His words were clipped. "I'm sure you're right, Erika." She beamed at his admission. "But I simply think the severe punishment of prison is wrong."

Her smile faded. "No bet?" she challenged.

"It's difficult for me to pass up such an inviting dare, but not this time. I'd be a fool to bet unless there's a chance to win, and I can't see any chance for the poor girl."

Alice winked at Erika, stood, and stifled a yawn. "It's after midnight, Mr. Parsons, and time for you to take me home."

Erika and Mitch walked with them to the door, saying goodnight. Mitch held out both hands. "Dance with me, Erika," he invited. She nodded sheepishly. In his arms, she felt his breath on her face and hair. This time, she didn't stiffen at his touch and they moved slowly to the music, relaxed and quiet. Erika wanted it to go on forever. She was lost in the feel of his warm solid body. The shelter it offered provided a defense allowing her release from everything but him. When the music stopped, she glanced into his eyes. He didn't move and they lingered.

Self-consciously, she moved away, taking his hand and

walking back to the table. Tiny pangs of pleasure rippled through her. Lost in euphoria, she slowly returned to reality. The sound of his voice brought her back. "I like your friends," he was saying. "Both of them are sharp. We kinda ganged up on you. Although you're probably right about Sara Bower, you didn't stand a chance against the three of us."

"I know. Arguments are for the courtroom. Actually I didn't want to argue with you. You were nice to let me off the hook."

He regarded her with a mocking smile. "A lawyer who doesn't like to argue. That's hard to believe. We're supposed to do it for fun and excitement."

"I'm best at it in the courtroom. It belongs there."

"We're supposed to argue," he insisted. "It's practice to hone our courtroom skills." He continued to smile. "You did surprise me about the Bower girl. I thought since she was female you would take her side. Most women do." He used his elegant pause again. "You're fighting me," he said, decidedly amused.

"I simply will not argue about arguing. It's foolish. Stop it," she ordered.

"Gotcha," he roared before they both laughed.

It was after two when Mitch unlocked her apartment door and insisted he go through it before she entered. After his inspection, he held her swaying to imaginary music. He kissed her forehead and murmured, "I enjoyed the evening and being with you. You'll be hearing from me again soon."

"It was a wonderful night," she whispered. "Thank you."

One friendly kiss on the lips and he was gone. Ten minutes later, she fell into bed, exhausted and happy, but sleep didn't come easily. Erika stared at the ceiling, watching the pictures of the evening in her mind. Inevitably, she returned to his remark that she was trouble. He was in no danger, she was. She'd never met a man like him—cavalier, jealous, successful, egotistic; a man with everything, and one who was evidently attracted to her. The timing was wrong. Bad timing, the scourge of the ages. According to her calculations, she needed two more years.

Two years! No way would Mitch Logan cool his heels for two years, and she couldn't throw away her career, not now.

It was seven when Erika decided no sleep was better than fitful sleep. She rolled on her side and kicked off the top sheet with her feet and stumbled to the shower hoping the water would revive her.

Showered and dressed, she stood by the window. The nearby park was almost empty, later it would be full of people escaping the heat of their apartments. She considered a walk. A brisk turn around the park might restore her energy since the shower failed. She stepped outside her door and locked it just as the phone rang. Glancing at her watch, she noted it was early for a call on Sunday morning. There was always a small hope it was Rick calling if the phone rang at odd hours. That dormant longing spurred her haste as she counted five rings before she answered a breathless "hello."

"Mitch Logan, Erika. Good morning. Sorry if I awakened you."

She felt foolish hoping the call was from Rick. She should know better by now. Reality returned swiftly. "It's okay. I've been up for a while. I'm surprised you're still in town. I thought you'd be on your way to Vail by this time."

"That's why I called. Go with me. We could have a picnic and escape a warm day in the city."

A stab of regret caught her, but she answered with conviction. "I can't. Tomorrow evening I begin teaching a contract law class. It's my first attempt at teaching, and I need to prepare."

"You can always work. Come with me," he pleaded.

"It's a tempting invitation, but I shouldn't."

"Bring your work. You can make your preparations and I'll attend a meeting I was willing to forgo if you said yes. I'll go to the meeting while you work and we'll still have plenty of time for a picnic."

She realized she was weakening. "I'd have to be back tonight, and you'd have to stay at your office again." She hated the way she sounded, because he could sense her resolve was fading simply by the sound of her voice.

"Bring your clothes for tomorrow. I'll have you in your office on time tomorrow morning."

Her face ignited. "I can't do that."

"Can you be ready in twenty minutes?"

"Will you bring me back tonight?"

He answered "Yes."

"I'll be ready," she croaked.

When Erika left her apartment, she was a few minutes early. She expected to wait, but not so. Mitch leaned on his car in an indolent fashion. "You're early," he called when she stepped out into the sunlight. "I was earlier, so I waited to give you your full allotment of time." Her insides did their usual flip at the sight of him. The natty jeans, checkered shirt, and reptile boots, plus his casual position, reminded her of a male model on TV. He separated from the Bronco. "I'm glad you decided to go. It's a beautiful day, too nice to waste being inside." He took her briefcase. "I'll put this in the back."

For a brief moment, Erika felt guilty choosing to fritter away the day playing instead of working. She climbed up into the Bronco. There was a kind of pleasure in permitting him to interrupt her plans and take over. After all, she worked hard, and for once, she wouldn't spend all day Sunday getting ready for Monday. She settled back looking forward to the rest of the day.

They followed the highway that trailed through the foothills into the spectacular, majestic Rocky Mountains. Erika tried to enjoy the scenery, but finally admitted to herself that she'd rather look at Mitch. She shifted slightly to face him. Without taking his eyes off the road, he said, "Tell me about this class you're teaching. You said contract law, didn't you?"

"It's one of those public service classes provided by the DBA. It isn't for college credit or anything. The course is designed for the layman."

He looked concerned. "Sometimes that's harder than teaching law students. At least they're familiar with the legalese."

"You may be right, but I hope not. Being a student is more my bag than being the teacher."

She noticed his smile widen. "How did you get roped into doing it?"

Erika laughed openly. "Don't ask. I was crazy enough to volunteer. Now I'm stuck with it."

He shook his head and glanced at her knowingly. "That I understand. I don't know how many times I've said yes to something similar and been sorry almost immediately."

"It isn't the first time for me either, but this mistake won't be too bad. The class only meets for the next three Mondays. Then it's over."

"Three weeks," he mused. "Long enough, and I wish you luck." She thought his face darkened, but they just rounded a curve and were in the shade of tall pine trees. She could be mistaken. Mitch negotiated several more curves before he spoke again. "How did you get mixed up in this crazy business anyway?"

"It's hard to say. As long as I can remember, I wanted to be a lawyer. I suppose it was the glamour that attracted me. When you're young, you don't think of the work it takes, not to mention the education."

"You did well in the education department. I know the DA's office only offers jobs to some of the top ten percent of D.U. graduates. You should be proud."

Erika wiggled. "When I consider my last year, I'm lucky I made it." She did it again, said something she wished she hadn't.

"Don't tell me you did what most students in their senior year do, fall in love and neglect their studies?"

The thought decidedly amused him. It would be easier to let him believe he was correct in his speculation. Knowing it was only an educated guess on his part didn't improve her predicament. "Sorry to disappoint you. Lack of money was the problem. I had to go to work in order to finish. That's why my last year lasted a year and a half." Erika didn't lie. Part of the money she reserved for school went to pay back Rick's employer in exchange for his dropping the charges against Rick. She couldn't tell that to Mitch.

"So money accounts for you choosing to work for the DA."

"Partly, but I thought it would be wise to investigate the role of a prosecutor before I began my own law practice. Give me two more years, counselor, and I'll be running you some competition."

He remained silent at her news. She turned to watch the scenery. His mocking voice was tinged with laughter. "I'll be looking forward to the competition, but I don't want to miss the chance of facing you in court in the meantime."

"Never mind," she said irritably. "I can wait."

"I'm sorry, Erika. I didn't mean to hurt your feelings or insult you."

"You didn't do either." She turned and smiled at him. "I just meant the more experience I have the better chance I have to be the winner when we meet in court."

The Bronco responded to his foot as he pressed down on the gas pedal. She sat up straight in her seat with her hands folded in her lap, watching the road in front of them. Obviously, the thought of losing didn't appeal to him any more than it did her. They rode and talked sparingly about the scenery. Later, Erika dozed. When she awoke, they were almost to Vail.

Before reaching town, Mitch turned off the highway onto a graveled road lined with trees. She sounded sleepy when she asked, "Where are we going?"

"My place," he replied. "It's not far now. You can get settled in and do your homework while I make the meeting in town."

She sighed. "Sunday meetings. Is that another price of fame?"

"Not this time. The owners of homes in this area are having a meeting to discuss a water shortage. I'm afraid we have outgrown our resources."

"Have you any idea how long you will be gone?"

He reached over and patted her knee. "An hour or two. Don't worry. You won't be alone. My housekeeper and her husband will be there."

Her head jerked and her eyebrows narrowed. "Your housekeeper?"

"I'm a mere man, Erika. I can't work and take care of a house myself." He was giving her a bad time, but just a small one. "Rosa and Enrique will make you comfortable."

The trees shaded the road and the air came through his rolled-down window cool and fresh. This place reminded her of a fairy tale, and she laughed quietly, thinking if the house were gingerbread, she'd roar. She caught her breath when they drove into a large clearing and she saw the big log house. It was much more than she anticipated. She had visions of a summer-type cabin. This was a large, imposing home. "It's lovely," she cried. "It's just beautiful."

Mitch turned off the engine. "Thanks, I built most of the original house. I'm glad you like it. We added the family room and greenhouse last summer. Rosa loves the flowers and vegetables and I like the solar heat. It pleases my billfold."

Erika cleared her throat. "May I go through your house? I would love to see everything."

Her request pleased him and he beamed. "Of course. Rosa loves company, and I'm sure she'll give you the grand tour." The front door opened and a small, thin gray-haired woman, forty-five or fifty, came out on the stone steps. "That's Rosa. Let her baby you and run the house and she'll be your friend for life." Mitch called to her and waved. He helped Erika from the Bronco and looked at his watch. "I'm sorry, but I am going to be late. Let me introduce you and run." He placed his arm about her shoulders and pulled her to him. "The sooner we get to work, the sooner we can get on with our picnic."

# *Chapter Four*

THE BEAUTY OF the house, its elegant simplicity, took Erika's breath away. She walked with Rosa from room to room in silence as Rosa cheerfully, and a bit boastfully, pointed out her personal favorites and related short histories of some of the furnishings.

The openness of the downstairs facilitated movement throughout, and except for the living room, the downstairs floors were dark brick to absorb the heat from the sun that streamed through large windows or glass doors. Erika heard the whirl of an unseen fan working to disperse the heat during the summer months, but in the winter, it would distribute welcome warmth throughout the house. She looked into the lush greenhouse where all sorts of plants and vegetables grew in different stages of development. Garden fresh tomatoes would be a treat in the winter, she thought. Indian blankets, sand paintings, and plants decorated the new family room. The furniture was oak and one very old quilt was displayed over the balustrade of the loft above, giving the room a quiet look. An antique pool table occupied the far end of the room under the overhang.

They climbed a stairway to the loft and the bedroom area. Twin couches were built at each end, separated by a huge table holding more greenery drinking in the sun from a skylight overhead. Erika walked around a Navajo rug decorating the gleaming hardwood floor. It was too striking to be walked upon, but her guide went across it without a second thought.

Beyond were three bedrooms, each with its own bath. Erika's interest centered on the master bedroom, Mitch's room. As she expected, everything was elegant, but the almost stark furnishings surprised her. The only apparent luxury was a magnificent moss-rock fireplace filled with wood waiting to be ignited. They passed quickly through the room to a balcony where the striking view and light, clean mountain air greeted them. The view was the only thing that could possibly surpass the house. A feeling of elation engulfed her. She spun around to Rosa. "You must love it here. It's gorgeous."

Rosa's answer was matter-of-fact. "My husband and I are fortunate to be here. We came four years ago when the house was almost finished." Erika couldn't understand why Rosa wasn't as overwhelmed as she. Turning around, she thought she would never take the beauty of this place for granted.

She looked over the balcony and spied the patio below with stone steps disappearing down into the trees. She asked, "Where do the steps lead?"

"Down to a stream. Mr. Logan fishes there when he has time. Do you fish?"

"Yes, but it was a long time . . ." The words to finish her statement died in her throat, as she remembered trips with her father and Rick. A sound from below brought her back to reality. She apologized. "I'm sorry. I was remembering the fishing trips with my father."

Rosa nodded. "You do a lot of remembering up here. It was a pleasant memory, I hope."

"It was," Erika replied. She leaned over the railing to get a better look at the patio, and what she saw brought a sparkle to her eyes. "You have a hot tub. I've never been in a hot tub. Is it as great as people say? It looks so inviting. Do you use it, Rosa?"

"Oh yes, miss. The tub is one of my favorite things around here. It's relaxing, and I like it best when it's cold and the snow falls. There's nothing like it; a warm steaming tub, the quiet, the snow and a glass of wine—you simply can't beat it."

The vision in Erika's head prompted her to laugh. "What happens when you get out of the warm tub on a snowy night?"

Rosa raised her eyebrows in an elaborate fashion. "You move

44

fast and you wake up quickly. You should try the tub before you leave. There are bathing suits, if you want to use one.''

"Rosa! Are you implying some people don't wear a bathing suit out there in the open?''

Rosa's eyes sparkled. "Nude is the only way, miss. Try it, you'll see.''

Erika felt a flame in her cheeks. Rosa saw it, and laughed. "Who will see you out here? If there's one thing we have plenty of, it's privacy. Anyway, there are suits. Do you want to try it now?'' Rosa asked.

She considered the offer, thinking Rosa either read her mind or she was too obvious with her desire to use the tub. "Not now,'' she answered wistfully. "I have some work to do. May I do it on the patio?''

"You go down and get started. I'll bring you some lemonade, then I'll prepare your picnic lunch.'' Rosa checked her watch. "When Mr. Logan returns, we want to be ready.''

"I'll be happy to help you with the food.''

Rosa waved off her offer. "The chicken is roasted. All I need to do is make the rice salad and pack the basket. Run along and see to your work.''

Downstairs, seated comfortably under a colorful umbrella, Erika demonstrated once more that when it came to work she could concentrate almost anywhere. She shut out all distractions, opened her mind, and let the ideas flow fast and furious. She finished in record time, and decided to explore a bit.

Her intention was to go to the stream, but as she descended into the dense trees, the sun disappeared and she stopped to adjust to the new light. She smelled the dampness of the earth and became entranced with the sounds of small creatures scurrying or flitting around her. She sat down and listened, watching intently. The forest was not as quiet as she believed. She stayed very still straining to hear and see what moved around her.

Later, when she heard Mitch call her name, she jumped up and ran to meet him. To her surprise, he pulled her to him and kissed her very thoroughly. His mouth was tender and warm. She felt her heart thump against his chest and every nerve became sensitive to his touch. She gasped when his mouth left hers. A smile crept over his lips which were still very near her own. "That's for getting all your work done. I assume you did, or you wouldn't be lazing around." His breath ricocheted off her face, making her skin tingle. "Ready for our picnic?"

Not trusting her voice, Erika nodded and took the basket. In a small clearing near the stream, Erika spread a blanket on the grass and opened the picnic basket. Mitch strolled to the edge of the water, selected his fishing spot and left his tackle box and fly rod. He returned and collapsed beside her. "I wonder what Rosa's made for us? I'm starved. I didn't eat breakfast this morning."

Erika dug into the basket. "I'm famished because I know what's in here." She lifted out a roast chicken, a generous container of rice salad, buttered rolls, and a bottle of white wine. "Are we expecting company?" she said. "No wonder this basket was heavy. Would you look at all this food!"

Mitch rubbed his hands together greedily and reached for the chicken. "Want to bet we eat all of it?" Erika was tempted to take the bet, but refused, shaking her head. Rummaging around, he pulled out flatware and plastic plates. He sounded truly alarmed as he asked, "Where're the glasses? I see the wine, but I don't see the glasses." He peered into the basket and breathed a sigh of relief as he pulled out two stemmed wine glasses wrapped with cloth napkins. "Rosa has class," he declared. "Now, let's hope she remembered a corkscrew."

Erika opened the lid wide, fully intending to search for a corkscrew, when she saw it fastened to the inside of the lid with a plastic tie. "Not only does Rosa have class, she's a clever lady."

They ate and drank with gusto. At the end of the meal, Mitch placed both hands on his flat stomach. "I couldn't eat another bite, but I do have room for one more toast." He raised his glass. "To Rosa, who prepared this feast, and to you, Erika, for making my day."

Erika acknowledged his toast with a nod and their glasses touched. "I would shout about what a wonderful day it is, but I'm too stuffed to risk it." Her smile was warm and her eyes misted. "I'm glad you called this morning. This is far better than my apartment."

Mitch kissed her cheek. "You're beautiful," he whispered. Erika's heart pounded. His tenderness touched her, yet it was difficult for her to accept his compliment. Her eyes wandered around the clearing as pink crept into her face and stayed. He lifted her chin to look at her. "Did I embarrass you?"

She swallowed hard. "A little."

"You shouldn't feel that way. You're beautiful and most women would kill to look like you."

"I like to hear you say it, but I guess I never thought much about it. I always considered myself average. Well, maybe a little above average."

He made no effort to hide his beguiling laughter. Finishing with a sputter, he ventured an observation. "If we had more wine, I'd drink to your idea of average, but I get the feeling you would bristle if anyone thought you were average in any way."

She looked resigned. "You're right." She wrinkled her nose at him. "And thank you for recognizing my beauty." A hearty bellow shook his body. Erika laughed with him. "You convinced me I'm beautiful, now you'll just have to live with my vanity."

He reached out and held her hand. "I think I'd like to do that." Embarrassed again, she pulled her hand away. After a slight pause, Mitch changed the subject. "Tell me, Erika, are there any more Wheatlys?"

Once again, she was grateful for his kindness. "My parents are dead. They died together in an accident about two-and-a-half years ago. I was still in law school at the time." She paused, contemplating whether or not to tell him about Rick. She decided this wasn't the time. Instead of continuing, she folded her hands and sat quietly.

"It must have been difficult for you."

"It was. Losing them both at once was a blow. I told you I had to go to work in order to finish my last year. That's why." A twinge near her heart forced her to acknowledge she wasn't entirely truthful.

"But you did well."

"The death of my parents hurt, and I buried myself in school and work to help relieve the pain. I became a workaholic."

"You told me about your plans for the future and I really do wish you luck, but remember Denver is full of attorneys; for that matter, the whole country is overstocked. The competition is tough. You'll need all your brains and beauty to get by." He looked down towards the stream. "But I'm sure eventually you'll make it."

She thought he sounded sad at the prospect. "Don't try to discourage me, Mitch. I know what you say is true, but I want it badly and I'm prepared to work for it."

"Does marriage and children have a part in your plans?"

She wiggled under his gaze. "Possibly. I haven't given much thought to marriage. There's plenty of time for a husband and children. I'm not over the hill yet." She met his smouldering stare and almost faltered. "One thing at a time. When my career is launched, then I can think of married bliss." Erika was positive the change in his expression was not a happy one. "Now let's talk about you," she said cheerfully.

Mitch shook his head. "You're more interesting."

She reached for the picnic basket and began to pack the dishes, searching for a way to tactfully change the subject. She felt ill at ease with the direction the conversation was taking. As she worked, she saw his fishing gear and tossed out a challenge. "If you catch a fish big enough, I'll cook it for you."

He rose and walked slowly to the stream. "Do you cook?"

"Yes, I can cook," she muttered under her breath, then answered him, "I'm no Rosa, but I get by." She watched as he prepared his fly-rod and began to cast. Erika lay on her stomach and rested her head on her folded arms. Ten minutes later he called to her.

"I haven't had a strike. Do you want to go for a walk?"

"I'm too content to move. Besides I like to watch you. You're very accomplished with the fishing rod." He smiled and threw out his line again. She yawned and rolled on her side. In only a few minutes, she fell asleep, a deep dreamless sleep.

Erika was catapulted from her repose by a strange, persistent, loud, clanging sound. She bolted upright as a shadow fell across her. Not remembering where she was, she panicked and struggled to her feet whimpering. Confused and frightened, she wanted to run, to get away from whatever was threatening her. As she scrambled to her feet, hands closed tightly around her waist and she bounced into Mitch's hard torso. His arms closed about her. Reality returned instantly and she nestled to him, listening to the strident noise, but now it sounded further away. She muttered, "What is that ringing?" No sooner had she asked than it stopped.

"Rosa," he replied lifting a hand to stroke her hair. "She has an old dinner bell. It's her way of calling us back to the house. It's time to go."

Her arms twined around his neck, and she felt his hair in her fingers. She sighed against his chest. "I wish you'd told me about the bell. It frightened me."

"I know. I didn't tell you because I thought we would leave in time to avoid it. Too bad you were awakened that way. You looked so peaceful and content, I didn't want to disturb you, and I didn't make it in time to rouse you." He laughed low. "I thought I could beat the bell, but I didn't."

She snuggled closer. "Why didn't you wake me? I shouldn't sleep on a beautiful day like this." He didn't answer, he just held her. "Do we have to go now?" she asked with considerable regret.

"Not this minute," he whispered, bending to seek her mouth. He wrapped her tightly in his arms. They didn't speak and Erika listened to their breathing and felt their heartbeats. She was totally and inexpressibly happy. When he kissed her the second time, she trembled, but heat filled her. Her lips parted, accepting his passion eagerly.

The mountain setting was special. Mitch was special. All the romantic ingredients were there. She gave in to the tenderness of his kisses, ignoring the warning flashing somewhere inside. It attempted to intrude on the glorious intoxication. There was no accounting of time or kisses when suddenly he held her away.

"Stay tonight with me." His eyes were dark with passion and he pleaded. "Please. Stay here tonight."

His words broke the spell and Erika began to fight the erotic feelings that threatened to overwhelm her. She shut her eyes to hide the longing glittering there. She didn't answer, but turned away from the glare of his burning eyes. She knew very little about this man, and it shocked her to realize she was considering his invitation. He wanted her and she wanted him. What a fool she'd been to let this happen. Knowing she encouraged the episode didn't make her feel any better. Without reason, she felt betrayed and cheap.

Mitch didn't wait long for her answer. Impatience was evident as he spoke. "It's all right, Erika." His hand came to rest on her shoulder. She shuddered at his touch, longing to be kissed once more. She fought the feeling. Why was this happening now? It's too soon. They were strangers. He increased the pressure of his hand. "Don't worry, Erika. Rosa will be ringing that damned contraption of hers again if she doesn't see us soon." He moved off the blanket, folded it and handed it to her. "You carry this and I'll bring the rest."

The blanket felt rough and damp in her hands. She tugged at it nervously, wondering why her reason had deserted her and why she had permitted raw passion to guide her. Still, looking at him as he bent to gather the last of their gear, she was ready to throw herself into his arms, but she saw his stern face. It was too late. "What happens if we don't show up?" she asked.

"Enrique is sent to search for us. Rosa doesn't lose anyone."

His answer was short and reserved. She looked around and noticed that the sun hung low over the mountain. She risked a smile. "It's time to go then. There's no reason for Rosa to launch a search." Before they reached the steps, she turned to him. "Please don't be angry with me?"

"I'm crazy for you, not angry."

Spirit gone and discouraged, she trudged ahead of him wondering why such a perfect day could end in this fashion. He was angry. She could see it in his face and tell by the way he moved.

They were halfway to Denver, and the tension between them hadn't relaxed. Any attempts at conversation had stopped, and his silence chilled the atmosphere. Erika experienced pangs of guilt, but it would embarrass her to try to explain she didn't want to be easy. She'd hate it if he thought of her as an easy mark. It was as simple as that. Yet it wasn't simple. Most of her life, through deeds and actions, her parents taught her to do what was right. His lovemaking was right in every way, but it was only their second date. Filled with remorse, she shrugged and rearranged her position to look out the side window. She heard his first attempt to clear his throat. The second was louder. He paused, drawing in air. "I shouldn't have come on so strong. Will you forgive me?"

She continued to watch the darkness. "I don't blame you. It wasn't entirely your fault," she murmured.

"I'm too tired to argue over blame. Shall we just forget it happened?"

"I'm not sure I want to forget," she told him honestly, turning her head as his right hand found her face and caressed it for a moment.

She saw a fleeting smile. In a perplexed and searching fashion, he asked, "What am I going to do about you?" She heard a low chuckle begin and slowly accelerate. He enjoyed his laugh before it stopped. "I've been turned down before, don't brood about it."

Erika chewed on her lower lip. Just looking at him raised her heart rate, but listening to what he said left her cold. She hugged her arms in front of her, warding off the chill. He'd set her straight. She wouldn't make the mistake of reading too much into their relationship again. "I'm not brooding. Let's forget it."

"We will after one word of advice. Be careful who you lead on in the future. Someone else might not be as easy on you as I."

She hung her head, hot at his insolent words, yet knowing there was an element of truth in them. "I've already accepted my part of the responsibility, and it's unfair of you to place all the blame on me."

"Perhaps," he mused, "but be careful. If I misunderstood the vibes, someone else could too."

She turned back to the window in a huff. "You sound like a father, not a . . . not a . . ." Her vocabulary failed. Intending to say "lover," she stopped, realizing her mistake.

"Not a what?" he demanded.

She noticed how quickly he pounced to take advantage of her confusion. "Never mind. It doesn't matter."

"It does to me," he insisted.

She leaned her head on the window and felt its coolness on her brow. "Forget it, Mitch. I shouldn't have compared you to a concerned father." She bit her lip again, but couldn't stop the spiteful words. "It's none of your business if I choose to lead a man on. If I want to, I will." She didn't know what she was saying, he had made her so angry.

"It is my business," he said flatly.

Erika floundered around in the seat, once more settling down and resting her head. What an aggravating man he was. Why should she parry with him anymore? He was better at it than she, and he always won or wore her down. She sulked openly, ending the conversation.

The lights of Denver sparkled in the night as the car descended into Golden, then suddenly disappeared. Mitch slowed the Bronco in the increased traffic. "I always hate this part of the trip,'' he complained. "It means tomorrow I'm back in the same old rut.''

It astounded her he would think he was in a rut. How could he, with the clients he had? Nevertheless, she offered some sympathy. "You're tired, and so am I. Your humor will improve in the morning.''

He acted as if he hadn't heard her. "This drive is too much. By September, October at the latest, I'm moving my office to Vail, and I can't wait.''

"What about your practice?''

"It'll survive, and if it does suffer, I don't care. I have more than I can handle now.''

"My guess is a move won't hurt you much.''

"You're probably right,'' he said with little regret.

"I really can't blame you. If I had your house, I wouldn't want to leave it either.'' The rest of the drive was spent in silence. Erika thought of the old adage, out of sight, out of mind, and hoped it might apply to her. It would be helpful if she weren't so available—helpful but lonely.

Before her apartment door, Erika made a clumsy attempt to test his temper. She cuddled to him.

He pushed her away. "Don't do that unless you're prepared to invite me in for the night.''

She kissed his cheek. "Goodnight, Mitch. The weekend was wonderful until we . . . Never mind,'' she added quickly. "I keep getting started wrong, for some reason. Thanks for asking me to your house. It's wonderful, and I love it.''

"Look,'' he said softly. "I'm sorry about this afternoon.''

She started to turn away. "It doesn't matter. . . .''

He forced her to face him. "But, it does.'' He stepped back. "Won't you accept my apology?''

"Of course,'' she answered.

"I hate to leave you like this. I don't want us to be at odds.''

She hadn't convinced him she was no longer angry. She wasn't angry about their romantic tryst, she was angry about his impossible attitude. "Oh, Mitch, I'm not mad. I'm exhausted.'' Her body ached from weariness, both mental and physical. "Why can't you just let it go?"

He pulled her to him and held her for a short time. "I'll be out of town most of next week, but I'll call you.'' From down the hall, he turned and waved.

Later, she sat on the bed, annoyed at herself and at Mitch. Her expression was grim. Mitch wouldn't call, she knew he wouldn't. Her world went topsy-turvy in just two days. One minute she was happy, the next, plunged to a new low. Turning back the sheets, she went to bed.

# Chapter Five

MONDAY, BY MIDMORNING, Erika was finding it hard to resist the urge to scream. Denver seemed to have gone mad over the weekend. The cause of the insanity was, of course, the summer heat. It claimed its toll in a hodgepodge of petty and serious crimes. Burdened with the process of sorting through the muddle, she had no time to think of yesterday, let alone worry about it.

On one of her hurried trips to Juvenile Hall, she met Josh and quickly agreed to spend Friday and Saturday evenings with him visiting some of Rick's old haunts and some other spots catering to teenagers. It had been two months since they looked for him. In a way, these forays frightened her, but she was always eager to go. If Rick was in Denver, they might get lucky and find him. To her, locating her brother was imperative, and Josh . . . well, Josh was a doll to give up his time to help her. How could she turn him down?

Erika left the feverish pace of the office for her law class at the community center with some apprehension, but her uneasiness proved unwarranted. As the class neared its end, she thought, all in all, it had gone well. The people who attended were serious business men and women who came because of a need or desire to learn. The two remaining classes would be a piece of cake. She left the building satisfied and walked outside into the warm, clear night.

A car door slammed and a man said "Hello." She couldn't mistake Mitch's deep voice. "I caught you quitting early. It's not ten yet."

"And I thought you left town."

"As you see, I didn't make it, but I'm leaving later tonight."
He took her arm and turned in the direction of the Bronco. "I
thought about you often today, and I couldn't go without seeing you." His arm slipped down to her waist. "May I buy you a
drink before I fly away into the night?"

His appealing smile dissolved any objections. Resting the
back of her head on his shoulder, she confessed, "Your timing
is fantastic. It's been a long day and a drink sounds delightful."

They drove to a neighborhood bar and chose to sit outside on
a wooden deck. The place was new, and she assessed the surroundings while he ordered. She wasn't sure how she felt about
Mitch. To be perfectly accurate, "ambivalent" was the best
descriptive word. When they weren't arguing, his eyes caressed
her and his nearness excited her, yet his self-serving attitude
perplexed her. But some incredible attraction drew her closer to
him with each new meeting. Everything about him was sensual;
tonight he looked sexier than usual. She watched his amazing
mouth as he talked. The waiter took their order and left and as
Mitch covered her hands with his, he asked, "Was it a good
day?"

"Yes, but very busy. I think the total population of Denver
ran amok over the weekend."

His eyes narrowed. "You look tired."

"Just a little." She moved her head to the side to escape his
eyes. His stare always made her feel uncertain and exposed.
"How was your day?" she managed to say.

"Wrapped up in my impending trip."

Erika pulled her hands from his and sat back in her chair. "I
suppose your trip is important?"

He made a small grimace. "Important to my client, but since
Saturday, I've wished I hadn't agreed to go. Nevertheless, I said
yes to it months ago and I can't back out now." He looked a
little sad. "I missed you today, Erika. I really did."

She suppressed a smile. "You sound as if missing me surprises you. Does it?"

He made a low chuckle. "I suppose it does."

After a short uncomfortable silence, Erika's curiosity got the better of her. "Where are you going?"

"San Francisco."

"Oh!" She lowered her head hastily and looked at the floor, hoping to hide her disappointment, but it was too late. Her "Oh!" gave her away. "I'm not used to people having clients everywhere." She moved slightly. "But San Francisco isn't far by plane, is it?" Judging by his smile, he enjoyed her addled state. "How long will you be gone?"

"A week, maybe longer."

The waiter delivered their drinks and Mitch paid him, telling him they wouldn't need anything else. He turned to her. "I have to be at the airport soon." He looked at his watch. "In just over an hour."

"What a pity. I hoped for more time with you than that." He dashed her expectations, but she had hidden it well.

"Come to San Francisco with me, Erika. I promise we'll have a great time."

He surprised her again. The invitation was totally unexpected. Loyalty to work and Rick surfaced, then vanished, and she experienced a strange urge to say yes without any reservation. Impatient with the signal that persisted within, she responded. "Don't ask me, Mitch. You know I work."

He straightened himself, his brown eyes watching. "Surely your job allows you some vacation. Take it and fly away with me."

Her head reeled. "You're leaving in an hour. It's impossible. I can't leave the office without notice and clothes and . . ."

"It's my plane. We could be a little late."

"No, no I can't." It seemed she always said no to him when she wanted to say yes.

"Of course you can, if you want. The world doesn't center around your job. Believe me, they'll manage without you. Say yes Erika, and we can be off quicker than you think." His eyes never left her as he spoke.

Mitch was a man who liked his own way. And was used to

getting it. There was no doubt about it. She struggled to find an acceptable and convincing argument for her side of the case. "Mitch, my vacation was in June. I can't expect them to give me time off now, and I told you the place is a zoo. I want to go, but I can't." His expression grew dark. "Surely you understand," she pleaded. "You have responsibilities, and you honor them just as I must."

His upper lip twitched and rose slightly. "Understanding and liking what I understand are different, my dear." He made a grunt of disgust and reached inside his coat and tossed a red and white envelope on the table. "Since you have crushed one dream, I'll try another. I was afraid you might refuse, so I bought this. It's an airline ticket. Join me Friday evening. At least we'll have the weekend together." Erika removed the ticket and pretended to examine it. Escaping one potentially dangerous situation, she found herself in the middle of another. Recovering from the shock of his second surprise, she almost missed the bitterness in his next words. "Please notice, you leave Denver long after a full day's work on Friday; you won't miss one minute of your duties, and you can be in San Francisco before ten, California time." He smiled. "That should settle the issue."

The idea that he was prepared for any answer but a complete refusal nettled her, and she closed her eyes to hide the hint of ire that flickered there. Her heart prodded her to go; it raced with anticipation. It'd be easy. One call to Josh and her weekend was clear, but could she live with herself wondering if she missed an opportunity to find Rick? Meeting Mitch's blunt stare was difficult and a chill trickled up her spine. "Sorry, but I can't go with you, not tonight or next weekend."

She thought he appeared amused. "Why not? I've taken the trouble to remove the major obstacle, your work. Whatever minor problems you have can be solved during the week. I'm certain of it."

Erika understood why it looked so simple to him, and she knew she ought to tell him about her brother, and how important it was to her to find him. She saw him take a hurried glance at his watch. But how could she rush an explanation about Rick? She couldn't, if she wanted him to understand. What was the use? No one understood about Rick but Josh. The timing was all wrong. Her throat tightened and she spoke with uncertainty. "Mitch, I have plans I can't cancel." She offered him the ticket and he wouldn't take it. Erika let it drop on the table, frustrated by her desire to please him and her inability to do what she knew she should. It was her fault. There had been opportunities for her to tell him, but she was ashamed of her brother's behavior and frightened Mitch would think less of her if he knew.

"If that's what you want," he seethed through his teeth.

Desperate, she snapped, "I didn't say I didn't want to go. I have an engagement I must keep, it's quite important to me."

"And I'm not. Is that what you're saying?"

"I'm saying I would like to go with you, but I have a commitment I must keep." His dour face caused her hand to find her hair and twist it. She groaned. "Why didn't you ask me last night?"

"Would it have mattered?"

"It might have," she told him.

His face grew hard, and his words were razor-edged. He called an end to the discussion. "You made your choice, and who am I to dissuade you?" He almost leaped from the chair. "I'll take you back to your car."

Before she stood, she whispered angrily, "What makes you so positive you're the only person in the world who could possibly have something important to do?" He said nothing, but his face stormed.

Sad and angry tears bedeviled her eyes on the short drive back to her car. Neither spoke a word. He stopped near her Chevette, moved toward her, then reached across and opened the door. She saw the deep furrow between his eyes in the dim overhead light. Her lips quivered. "Why can't you understand?" He remained silent and his brown eyes seemed to look through her.

The Bronco didn't move for as long as she could see it in her rearview mirror driving away. Erika analyzed her behavior and agonized over the results. Facing the bottom line, she knew the main reason she didn't tell Mitch about Josh and the coming weekend was that she was mad. Mitch Logan had an uncanny ability to make her furious.

Two weeks passed. Erika continued to expect Mitch to call. At the end of the third week, she no longer thought he might call or appear in a doorway. The fourth week came and went and she had no hopes at all for a reconciliation. She missed him terribly, and at the same time rationalized it was best they went their separate ways. Strange how they were so eager to be together; yet, together meant tension and disagreement. But what use was worrying about it? It didn't matter now.

Erika's life was much as it had been before, maybe a bit blander. Rick was still missing. Her job continued to be demanding, but interesting. She didn't see as much of Alice since Ted Parsons was on the scene, but she could count on Josh. He didn't desert her. They continued to meet and have their lazy dinners and go on the town looking for Rick as the dog days of August came and went, ushering in September.

It was nearly midnight on the fourteenth when the phone jangled her from sleep.

"Josh Manning, Erika. I've found Rick."

Dazed and more asleep than awake, all she heard was the name of her brother. It passed through her mind that this wasn't Rick. "Who is this?" she mumbled through a husky throat.

"Erika, it's Josh. Wake up and listen. I've found Rick."

His words registered and the transition from sleep to awareness was immediate. "Rick? My God, where is he?"

"Here in Denver. I'm sending Officer Dave Glass to take you to him. You know Dave, don't you?"

"Yes I do, but . . ."

"Get dressed and meet him out front."

Josh hung up before she could ask any of the many questions forming in her mind. Her hands shook, making it difficult to dress and almost impossible to apply makeup. She settled for lipstick and rushed from the apartment forgetting the anger she sometimes felt toward her brother. The prospect of seeing him again overshadowed everything.

Dave's face was sober, and he turned away when she crawled into the patrol car. His look after the hellos caused her to suspect something was wrong. His fingers tapped the steering wheel nervously. His jaw was set and his mouth tight. "Your brother . . . Rick . . . is in the hospital, Denver General. We need you to make a positive ID."

"What?" Erika's voice rose precariously. He began to repeat his words. She interrupted. "Why? Why, Dave?"

He wouldn't meet her eyes and drew in a deep breath, letting it out slowly. "There was a robbery at a drugstore on East Colfax. Someone inside the store tripped a silent alarm, and Josh and his partner, Patrolman Jackson, were close. They answered the call. The two kids inside saw them and ran out of the store. During the chase, your brother fired a gun at Jackson. He missed, but Josh didn't. He says he shot your brother. I don't know much more about it, but Josh told me to tell you he's sorry."

She grasped at anything. "Maybe it isn't Rick?"

He shook his head. "Don't get your hopes up. The kid with him said he was Rick Wheatly."

Erika couldn't believe what she heard. Rick must be dead. That was it! Rick was dead. Her brain ceased to function further. "Is he dead?"

"I don't know," he answered quietly. "He was alive when they put him in the ambulance, but he's in bad shape. Josh wanted to be here, but he'll be tied up for a long time with questions and reports."

She was going out of control. She heard it in her voice, and she felt it in the coldness creeping through her body. Losing the battle to fight down the panic, she whispered, "Take me to him," and slumped in the seat. Immediately, the wheels of the car squealed and skidded into the street. Erika was numb. The siren above her seemed far away, and the flashing lights made eerie shadows dance around her.

The hospital was uncommonly busy for the time of night. She waited, cold and afraid, as Dave talked to someone at the desk. Dave showed his badge, and the woman pointed down the hall to the right. They walked swiftly to the elevator and started down. "Where is he?" she choked in a voice laden with emotion.

"In emergency. That's good, he's still alive."

Inside a small curtained room, Erika saw her brother for the first time in two years. Stunned at his appearance, she wasn't sure she recognized him. He was ashen and emaciated, his long blonde hair matted and stiff. It was Rick, but not the brother she remembered. Carefully, her hand went to his face and rested there. She leaned backward on Dave for support. "It's him," she whispered ever so quietly. Dave's body trembled against hers. He stepped back and groaned. "I'm sorry."

Dave stayed until Rick could be moved to a room and Alice had arrived, responding to a call Dave had made for Erika earlier. Both women waited silently, interrupted only by nurses who checked on Rick regularly. Sometime during the night, Erika's hopelessness was replaced by anger and the anger turned to frustration. No one had any control over what was happening.

Rick Wheatly died at ten in the morning and the remainder of that day and the next were forever a blur in Erika's memory.

When the graveside service was over, Alice and Erika went to the limousine. Erika remembered that when her parents died she swore she would never ride in another one of those cars. Just before Erika started to get in, she saw Mitch standing away from the group watching her. She walked over, stopping a few feet in front of him, and tried to smile bravely. "Hello, Mitch. Thank you for coming." She stopped, expecting to say more, but couldn't.

He made no effort to touch her. "I only found out this morning. I've been out of town. I'm sorry, Erika." They stood for a long moment looking at the other. His eyes searched hers, intending to read her thoughts. He did. He knew exactly what she was thinking. He held out his arms and she rushed into them. He held her with one hand on the back of her head, pressing her to his body. Although there were no tears, she sobbed silently. "Can I do anything for you?" he said.

She struggled against tears. They were always hiding just below the surface ready to overflow. Controlling them was almost too much. Seeing Mitch was almost too much. If she looked at him, she'd blubber. She backed away and looked in his direction, but not at him. "No, but my friends have prepared lunch for anyone who would like to come. It's at my apartment. Would you like to come?"

"If you want me . . ."

Her strained face met his. "Yes."

"Go along with Alice. I'll be there soon." His eyes looked so sad. She wanted to tell him to hurry, and say that she was all right, but it was impossible.

Her apartment was crowded with people talking in hushed tones and eating. Dick Renquist handed her a cup of coffee. "You should find a place to sit and drink this. You look exhausted."

"I'm fine," she replied, wondering how many times she had said those words in the past two days.

"You don't look fine. I don't want to see you back at work too soon, not until the middle of next week for sure."

"Today's Thursday. I can't take the week off." She watched the door, waiting for Mitch. "I'll be there Monday. Right now I need to keep busy."

Renquist frowned. "You may be right, but take care, Erika.

If you get sick, I'm minus one of my best assistants. Don't do that to me.''

She ventured a smile. Everyone was being kind. A devil inside her wished they'd stop. The kindness was one reason the tears lurked in her eyes. It became necessary for her to change the subject. ''Mitch Logan said he would come by.''

''Good. I haven't seen him for over a month, and I expected him to come. You two are good friends, aren't you?''

''For a while we were,'' she answered. Afraid of the turn in the conversation, she retreated to the kitchen. When she returned, Mitch was shaking Dick's hand. They exchanged a few words and he came to her, his eyes boring into hers. ''You're all right, aren't you?''

''All right doesn't quite describe the way I feel, but I'm making it.'' She shrugged. ''I feel so empty.''

''My offer to help still stands.'' He bent to kiss her cheek. ''Anything I can do, I will.''

Her voice quivered. ''Please stay if you can. I feel safer when you're near.''

He nodded. ''You have me for as long as you want.''

Mitch kept her under his watchful eye; for the next hour, he was never more than a few feet away. Neighbors and coworkers came, expressed their sympathies and left. One by one they filtered quietly from the apartment leaving Mitch and Alice. Erika closed the door behind her last guest, looked at Alice and shuddered. ''Since I hadn't seen Rick for two years, I thought this would be easier than it was with my parents.'' She shook her head. ''It wasn't.''

Alice hugged her and walked her to a chair at the kitchen table. ''You've done remarkably well, my friend. I'm proud of you.''

Erika looked at Mitch. Tears glistened. ''When Alice is nice to me, you know the situation is grim.'' She meant to laugh, but the noise came out more like a sob.

Alice continued to be kind. ''Do you want something to eat? You haven't eaten today.''

"Later," she answered wearily. "Right now, I just want to sit."

Alice spoke to Mitch. "Can you stay with Erika for a couple of hours? I'm in court tomorrow and I need time at the office. I would appreciate it if you could."

Mitch nodded. "Take all the time you need. I'll be here when you get back."

The door scarcely closed behind Alice when Erika stood and looked around the kitchen. "Come on, counselor, we ought to clean up." They both looked at the mess.

"Leave it," he pleaded. "You need rest. When did you sleep last?"

"I'd rather stay awake. When I sleep, I have nightmares, and that's no rest. I want to keep busy. It keeps me from dwelling on everything." Erika took his hand and pulled him toward the sink.

He removed his coat and rolled up his sleeves, giving her a disapproving look. "Someone should've done this for you." He slipped by her and started to empty the sink.

A semblance of a smile appeared on her face. "Someone's helping. You." She brushed around him and handed him a towel. "Tie this around you or tuck it under your belt. It'll save your handsome suit."

Soon, the assembly line they formed operated efficiently; he washed and she dried. It crossed her mind that Mitch was no stranger to the kitchen. Absorbed in the task, they worked for a while before he spoke. "Is Alice really in court tomorrow?"

"Probably, and I know what you're thinking. She did leave in a hurry. Alice has been very kind and that's what matters. I think she just had to get away for a while. Who could blame her? I wish I could leave too."

He continued to wash dishes. "I know she's staying with you tonight, but what about the weekend?"

Erika sighed. "I don't know. I can't think that far ahead." She put a stack of dishes in the cabinet. "Did Alice tell you about the funeral?"

65

"No, I read it in the paper. I returned from Washington late last night, and I read the announcement in the *News* this morning."

She groaned loudly. "I forgot about the papers." Mitch stopped washing to observe her. "Don't look at me that way, Mitch Logan," she ordered. "The whole sordid mess has been in the papers, hasn't it?" She rushed to answer her own question. "Of course it has, a robbery and a shooting!" She threw the towel on the floor. Painful tears sparkled in her eyes.

"Don't, Erika, it . . ."

"Don't *don't* me. How would you like it if your family problems were printed for everyone to read? Would you want the world to know your brother was a thief?" She picked up the towel and dried a few more dishes, stacking them with a sharp clack.

"Your brother was responsible for his actions, not you. There's no reason for you to be ashamed."

She twisted the towel with her hands furiously. "Who's ashamed?" She stopped wringing the cloth and glared at him. "For two years, I have told myself Rick was a good kid, but he was a petty hood. You don't know how hard that is for me to accept. I'm ashamed of what he did." She hesitated. "All you know is the ending of the story. Keep washing and I'll tell you the beginning." Erika began slowly and told him the story, including her searches with Josh. She spoke with detachment and Mitch listened in silence. When she finished, she looked at him sternly. "Don't you ever tell Alice that Rick took money from the garage where he worked. She doesn't know about it and I don't want her to know. She'll just feel sorrier for me than she does."

Mitch removed the towel and dried his hands on it. He cupped her face with his hands, holding her so she could not turn away. "It doesn't matter, Erika." He pulled her into his arms with gentle firmness. She was glad he didn't tell her not to cry. The tears she'd been fighting for days rolled out of her eyes and down her cheeks. He held her and let her cry.

Later Mitch made them a drink and they sat in the living room on the couch. She was talking about her family when suddenly she found herself saying, "You came back when I needed you. I won't forget it, Mitch."

His finger ran up and down the glass he held. His expression was unreadable and his voice deliberate. "When I stormed away a few weeks ago . . ."

She corrected him. "It's been over six weeks."

His mouth twitched and his brown eyes cleared. He seemed reluctant to say more. "This is no time to talk about our last meeting." He shifted to look at her. "Well, maybe it is. I was angry and hurt. I didn't know you had problems. I admit your work interfering with our pleasure galled me, and after you refused my weekend offer without a satisfactory explanation, I thought there was someone else. How could I know the someone was your brother?" His head moved slowly from one side to the other. "Staying away from you has been hard; one of the most difficult challenges I've ever met."

"I should've told you about Rick earlier."

He nodded his agreement. Suddenly Erika felt exhausted. She yawned and bent her head to his shoulder. "You didn't slip me a Mickey, did you? I'm very tired."

"Come here," he muttered and arranged her body to rest close to his. She buried her head in the hollow of his neck, savoring the protection he provided. "You're sad and frightened. Close your eyes and rest."

Later, she roused when he carried her to bed, removed her shoes and covered her. "Don't go," she pleaded.

"I won't. Now sleep."

It was nine when she stumbled into the kitchen, half asleep. Alice and Mitch sat at the table drinking coffee.

Alice greeted her. "You're up. Come have coffee with us?"

"No thanks, it might keep me awake," she joked in a low thick voice. "I can't believe I slept so long." She tilted her head at Mitch. "Are you certain there wasn't something in that drink?"

Mitch beamed at her and held up his hand. "Only booze and water. I swear. You needed the rest or you wouldn't have slept so well."

Erika took a glass from the counter, went to the refrigerator and poured a glass of milk. She held up the carton. "Anyone else?" Both shook their heads. She sat down with them and they talked, avoiding the reason they were there together.

Mitch rose and offered his hand to Erika. "It's after ten. Walk me to the door. You'll get more sleep if I'm not in the way." He spoke to Alice. "It's kind of you to stay with Erika tonight."

Alice smiled. "And I'm glad you came."

Erika hated to see him go. At the door, she stood on tiptoe and kissed him. "Thanks for being here. Talking about Rick helped." His arms surrounded her and held her. His kiss was soft and warm. He let go of her and headed for the door, then turned and looked at her. The moment wasn't strained, but tender, and his look sent a small twinge of regret through her. "I've missed you, Mitch," she said warmly.

"I've missed you. Take care, Erika." She leaned on the door after it closed, thinking how kind he could be.

"He's a nice man," Alice said when she returned to the kitchen. Erika sat down, feeling strangely remote from her surroundings. Alice eyed her. "What's wrong?" she asked, genuinely concerned.

Erika shook her head, "Nothing. I felt a little dizzy, that's all. It's gone now."

Alice looked at her, unable to hide her amusement. "The cause of your malaise just walked out the door. He's not gone for good. Don't worry, he'll be back."

"What makes you so sure?"

"The man loves you, Erika, and that's a fact."

"Alice . . ." Erika stopped her reply. Even if her friend was right, she couldn't deal with it now. She walked into the hall and returned with a brown leather photo album. "I want you to see some pictures of my family."

Alice appeared embarrassed. "Maybe this isn't the right time to do this."

Erika sat next to her and opened the book. "It's the best time I can think of. It will remind me of happier days."

# Chapter Six

A STIFF BREEZE blew in Erika's face and she pulled her light jacket around her neck and held it closed. The idea of a whole day stretched out before her without any purpose set her running for the park to think and plan. After Alice left for work, she cleaned the apartment and completed chores usually reserved for weekends, then wandered around for a while brooding about events that were better forgotten. Enough time had been allowed for grieving. In many ways, it had already lasted for two years. She must begin at once to reconstruct her life. Yet, she failed to put aside one queston about Rick, and it continued to haunt her. How could Rick be a normal, likeable boy for fifteen years, then change so drastically? It didn't make sense, and though there was no reason to expect she'd ever find the answer now, the question wouldn't go away.

The whole summer had been a disaster, except for Mitch. He stumbled into her life accidentally, taking charge and changing her. Was Alice right? Did he love her? A warm euphoria came over her, just thinking about him. She found herself reliving the scene near the stream and flinched, ashamed to have such thoughts and desires now.

Heading back to her apartment, she thought of Josh. She hadn't seen him at the funeral. The realization that she didn't know what to think about Josh anymore triggered a shiver starting in her center and spreading to her arms and legs. Erika hurried inside.

She made herself a sandwich for lunch, but after two bites left it on the table and curled up on the sofa to watch TV. Instead, she found herself watching the clock and listening to the muted sounds outside the apartment. She wished she'd gone to work, even if Dick wouldn't approve. Sitting with nothing to do was much worse than being busy. Caught in a limbo of conflicting emotions, she failed to hear the doorbell until it rang the third time. She jumped to answer it. It had to be someone to talk with, if only for a moment.

Mitch was turning to leave when she opened the door. He heard the sound and wheeled around. "Erika, I thought you were gone. I'm glad I was wrong." She stood aside and motioned for him to come in. He took her face in his hands and moved his thumbs under her eyes. Her heart began to thump. "The dark circles are still there. Poor dear. You're not sleeping well, are you?" He didn't expect an answer and he kissed her before he closed the door. "I need to talk to you. Are you up to it today?"

She smiled and took his hand, leading him to the couch. "Please talk. You're a welcome sight. I was debating about going to work . . ."

"You weren't," he exclaimed impatiently.

She nodded. "Yes, I was. It's lonesome and I could use something to do." They stood facing each other. His eyes held hers. Stirred by his inquiring gaze, Erika looked away to relieve the strain she felt. "Sit down, Mitch. Can I get you something?" she said softly.

"All I need is you." He tapped the sofa. "Sit with me."

Erika had become more wary than usual this past week and he seemed subdued. "You're not bringing me more bad news are you?"

"No, at least, I don't think so. Sit down. I want you close to me." She felt a warm cozy feeling returning as she settled down beside him. He took her hand.

She looked relieved and sighed. "Tell me, counselor, what's on your mind?"

He faced her. "Can we talk about Josh Manning? Be honest, now. If it's going to upset you, it can wait."

72

With little enthusiasm and a slight wrinkle of her nose, she answered. "I can think of better subjects, but it's okay."

Mitch shifted his weight. "Something has happened you should know about before you get hit with it when you return to work Monday."

"What is it?" she demanded, perceiving a kind of electricity in the air. "Remember, you said it wasn't bad news."

His eyes questioned her. "Josh Manning came to see me today. There's going to be a grand jury investigation of the shooting to determine if charges should be brought against him."

Eyes wide, she stammered. "I . . . I don't understand. There's always an internal investigation when a police officer shoots someone. It should be over and done with by now."

He shifted around again. "It is, but Josh wants me to represent him for a further investigation." He rushed on. "Does Josh Manning know we're friends?"

"He may," she answered, still wondering, Why the additional investigation? "But I didn't tell him." She was completely confused. "Mitch, I don't understand why Josh needs a lawyer and why he'd choose you. He can't afford you."

"You didn't recommend or refer him to me?"

"No. I haven't seen or talked to him since before . . ." She stopped, not wanting to finish, then went immediately to the point. "There's a problem with the shooting, isn't there?"

Mitch hung his head. "It appears so, but remember how many shootings there've been this summer. There've been some rumblings about police brutality, and it's up to the DA's office to squelch them. Your office asked for the grand jury. They may want to make everything open to the public because you're employed by the DA."

Erika pushed the hair from her eyes, shuddering at an inner stab of uncertainty. "The department's internal investigation usually settles these situations. I take it, it didn't."

"Manning said it didn't, and I haven't had the chance to talk with the DA—not that he'd tell me anything."

She braced for her next question. "What's wrong?"

Openly distressed, he replied, "Let's forget about it. I was stupid to bring it up. You aren't ready for this yet. I didn't dream you'd view this as ominous or threatening, but since you do, I won't pursue it."

"Don't try to pass it off as if it never happened. I want to know what's wrong with the shooting. There wouldn't be an investigation unless something was wrong."

"I don't have any details, and if I did, I couldn't tell you. If I take Manning's case, you're the enemy."

Her voice rose. "If you take the case? You wouldn't!" When he didn't answer, she turned to look at him with cold eyes. "Discuss it with me. When I get back to the office, I'll find out about it anyway." He stood and strolled around the room. Her eyes followed him as he circled the sofa and stood before her.

"I'm a defense lawyer, Erika, and a damned good one. It's my job to take cases like this one, but I won't if it's going to cause trouble between us. I've found you again and I don't want to risk losing you."

She turned from his prying eyes. "Surely you aren't asking my permission?"

"It isn't a matter of permission. I don't want to add to your problems. I'll refer Manning to another attorney, if you want."

Once again, the two of them were trapped on opposite sides of an issue. "It doesn't take a mind reader to know the DA suspects the shooting might not be clean, or he wouldn't call for a grand jury. Rick was my brother." She stopped to gather herself. "What do you want me to say?"

He sat down and took her hands. "Listen, and try to understand. The investigation is for the public. It's a show and mostly political. The DA gets his name in the paper, Manning is cleared, and the people of Denver have confidence in their police again. That's all it is."

"You sound so certain."

"I am."

"And what about Josh? His feelings aren't important? He's a good officer, and if this is just politics, it shouldn't happen."

"That's exactly why he needs me. I could make it easier for

him. When I met him, he impressed me. I'm not easily impressed after all my years in this business. He's clean, Erika.'' She looked at Mitch, not at all convinced he was right. She heard the twinge of resignation in his voice. "Tell me about Manning. How well do you know him?"

"He investigated a case for me just after I went to work. We worked together on others over the months, and he does excellent police work. From that, we drifted into a friendship. Other than he's good at his job and he was kind to me, I don't know too much about him." She withdrew her hands from his. "I told you yesterday how he helped me try to find Rick."

It seemed ages before he spoke. Except for a spark in his eyes, his face was markedly expressionless. "Do you love him?" Stern brown eyes watched her.

"No! We're only friends." She stood and took a few quick steps to put distance between them. "How can you even ask that?"

"Strictly friends?"

His insistence rankled her. "We had an easy, relaxed friendship, but it'll be a long time, if ever, before I'll be comfortable with him again."

Mitch motioned for her to come back to the sofa. "I'm sorry, Erika, but I had to ask. If Manning is in trouble, I must learn everything I can about him. The hearing won't be a whitewash, even if Josh is just a victim of the summer madness. After the grand jury makes its decision, I'm certain everything will be okay."

She sat down. "Did Josh tell you anything about the shooting?"

"No. We only had time to talk about me taking the case. I'm to call him this afternoon and give him my answer. From what you say about his police work, he shouldn't worry."

Erika sighed. "Well, he's entitled to the best defense he can find. That's you."

"Oh God, Erika, your legal training is talking. What does your heart say?"

Her answer was swift. "My heart tells me to beware of the

whole mess. You'll have to accept a legal answer or none at all. If he wants you, and you want to take the case, I won't interfere."

"You don't think he intentionally killed Rick, do you?"

"He didn't know Rick. He had no motive." She thought back to the night Rick died and the recollection made her squirm. The pain of remembering prompted her to make a face. "No. I don't believe Josh intended to shoot him."

Mitch spoke softly. "Do you want him to be a sacrificial lamb for the city? It's possible."

"No," she whispered.

"Then, it's settled. You won't be angry with me?"

She smiled. "So what if I get angry with you. I can't stay angry for long." The words barely slipped out before she regretted them, but she could tell Mitch wanted to defend Josh. Erika wondered if the time would ever come when they wouldn't be adversaries. "Can we talk about something else now? I've about had it with this conversation."

He placed his hand on her face and caressed it. "I have just the right change in mind. Come to Vail with me for the weekend."

She put her hand on his. "I was beginning to think you'd never ask." They both smiled and he kissed her. Erika pulled away. "Will you promise we won't talk about Rick or Josh?"

"I promise," he said and kissed her again. He raised his eyebrows saying a silent "wow." "You pack and I'll call Manning and tell him he has a lawyer." Her sly glance caught his self-satisfied expression. She experienced a prickle of fear beneath her skin as she left the room.

A weekend with Mitch in the mountains was what she needed. For two days, he kept her so busy she succeeded in forgetting her problems. Rosa prepared such delicious and tempting meals, her appetite returned, and the magic of the hot tub soothed her jittery nerves. She slept without dreams.

Late Saturday night, they returned from dancing to the

luxury of the hot tub. He held her in his arms in his special way. His warmth and the whirling water sent tremors dancing wildly through her and she nestled tightly to him. "You drive me up the wall," he whispered, his voice shaking. His demanding kiss excited every nerve, and more warmth crept into each recess of her body. With every kiss her hands clung to him tighter. He looked at her and she was lost in his smouldering gaze. Erika wilted in his arms choked with passion. His kisses grew more demanding, wordlessly telling her, this time he wouldn't allow her to escape his desire. A small cry of protest came from her as he lifted her out of the tub and carried her toward the bedrooms. She rested her head on his shoulder, her ardor untouched by the cool night air.

He said nothing, but hurried to her door where he placed her on the floor. He held her tightly, murmuring into her hair. "You marvelous sexy woman," he breathed, and stepped back to look at her. Then, turning quickly, he headed down the hall. "Hurry," he said. Mitch disappeared into his room, leaving the door open. Her delight evaporated, as she faced the choice to follow or not. His invitation was obvious, and her anxiety increased. Yet the sight of him going down the hall forced her to think rationally. Sadly, she entered her room, and later as she tossed in bed, still longing for him, she heard his door close.

Sunday morning, clouds hovered over the valley. Now and then a hardy snowflake would make it to the ground while the others melted during their descent. Mitch and Erika lingered over their breakfast until almost noon. Neither mentioned the night before. He sat back in his chair, smiling the small crooked grin she loved so much. "I was going to take you fishing today, but the weather isn't cooperating. It's too cold." His brow creased into a question. "How about a movie instead?"

"Okay, but promise me you'll get me back to Denver early. I'm going to work tomorrow and I need to be ready for it." She waited for his objections.

"Deal," he said reaching out to caress her hand. "I agree you should go back to work. You're much happier when you have something to do. Besides, you look much better now.'' Erika wondered if she would ever learn to read his mind as he could hers.

The movie was rated ''R'' for rotten and they chose not to go. After drifting around the village, Mitch drove her to Denver and bought her dinner. Afterwards, he helped her settle in her apartment, then plopped down on the sofa, refusing her offer of a drink. He pulled her down on his lap. ''I neglected to tell you today you're beautiful.''

Erika snuggled. She savored the feel of his strong arms around her. ''Tell me more. I love to hear . . .'' His arms tightened around her and his mouth stopped her words. Always aching for his kiss, her mouth opened to his, and she tried to concentrate on keeping control of her growing desire. Each time he held her, it grew more difficult. Pulling his mouth from hers, he studied her closely. ''You'd consider letting me stay tonight, wouldn't you?''

The erotic tension and frustration were unbearable and delectable. A tortured groan escaped her throat and the sound brought her back from the vortex that had her spinning. Taking his hand and kissing it, she shook her head to answer him.

In one swift movement, he stood her on the floor. She heard the strain in his voice as she rested her head on his chest, listening to the sound of his heart. His words were curt. ''Don't wave the banner of morality at me. You want me to make love to you almost as badly as I want to.'' He sighed and seemed resigned. ''I was unkind. Forgive me.'' He kissed her gently. ''I'll see you tomorrow, Erika.'' She watched him leave, consumed with longing, wanting him to come back and make love to her. Why did he listen to her?

Erika was fifteen minutes late when she rushed into her office, expecting to find mountains of work waiting for her. Instead, she saw the top of her desk quite bare. Back outside her door, she searched for Rhonda, who was nowhere in sight; she strode impatiently to Dick Renquist's office, and he wasn't in.

Nothing was working in her favor. She wanted to talk to Dick about Josh, and find out as much as she could about the grand jury.

"Hi, Erika," Rhonda called when she rounded the corner, returning to her office. "Glad to have you back, but I didn't know you'd be in today."

"No one seems to be in. Where's everyone?"

"In court, mostly." Rhonda held up a coffee mug. "Want some?"

Erika shook her head. "Who's doing my work?" Rhonda followed as they walked into Erika's office.

"Different people. We spread it around." She caught her breath. "And before you ask, Mr. Renquist will be out for most of the day."

Erika sat at her desk spreading her hands to indicate nothing was there. "I need some work. I can't sit here all day." Rhonda didn't appear sympathetic. "Bring me the file on Josh Manning. That's a good place to begin." Rhonda didn't move and Erika looked at her. "The Josh Manning file," she repeated carefully.

"The only way you can get that file is to ask Mr. Renquist. He's keeping it under lock and key." Rhonda licked her lips. "There's a memo out. We can't discuss the Manning case with you."

"Who is 'we'?" Erika demanded.

"Any of us here in the office. Do you want to see the memo?"

Erika released her breath slowly. "Not now. I can guess what's in it, but when you have time, leave a copy on my desk. Is it against orders for you to tell me who's handling the Manning case?"

Rhonda shrugged. "Renquist. Who else?"

Erika permitted a wry smile. "What am I to do then? Since my first day here, I've never had an empty desk."

"I'd go home and read a good book, if I were you. You may never get the chance again."

"Big help, Rhonda," Erika complained, then smiled. "Wait a minute. You've given me an idea. I'll be leaving the office for a while. In the meantime, see if you can find something for me to do." She took a note pad and her purse and rushed from the room. Since Renquist was concerned about her connection with Rick and Josh, she'd have to find out as much as she could on her own. She thought of Mitch. Did the DA know he represented Josh? Considering everything, Renquist was probably right to keep her out of it. With a small smile of admiration for her boss, she left the building.

At the library, Erika read the news accounts of her brother's death. The reading was painful, but she scoured all the articles. She scribbled notes, including the address of the drugstore and the name Ty Kimball, the boy who was with Rick when he was shot.

On impulse, she drove to the run-down neighborhood and located the drugstore. Five school-age boys gathered on the corner and watched her. Two buildings on the block were boarded up, plastered with large red signs reading DANGER and KEEP OUT. A dilapidated one-story apartment across the street was the only possible place anyone might have seen what happened. She pulled into its parking area and cautiously followed a sign leading her to the manager's office. She knocked three times before a large, gray-haired woman smelling of beer answered, demanding, "Whatcha want?"

"My name is Erika Wheatly. "I'm from the district attorney's office. I'd like to ask you some questions about the shooting that took place here on the night of the fourteenth."

The old woman bristled and huffed. "I told everythin' to the cops. I didn't hear nothin' and I didn't see nothin', neither. In this place, you get to where ya don't pay no never mind." She huffed again. "Now git and stop botherin' me." She slammed the door.

"Please . . ." Erika cried, but the door remained closed. The atmosphere was hostile, and Erika wanted to leave. Making an inarticulate sound, she glanced around, taking in the details of this depressing place. The boys on the corner seemed to be watching her more intently now. She left, glad that, at least, Rick hadn't died here.

Disappointed that her trip was for nothing, she headed back to the office. Erika kept thinking about the boy with Rick, Ty Kimball. She wanted to talk to him, but there was little chance. No doubt he'd been assigned an attorney, and she would need that attorney's permission to see him. And what about Renquist? He would have a bird if she found a way to talk to Kimball. Considering the complications that could arise, other than defying Dick, she turned at the next corner and drove to Juvenile Hall.

"I'm from the DA's office," she told the large sergeant behind the desk. "I want to see Ty Kimball."

He held out his hand without looking up from the magazine he read. "ID?" She handed him a plastic card. He scrutinized it and looked at her from under his glasses. She trembled at her boldness and his stare. He pointed across from them to a door at the end of the hall. "Wait in the last room. I'll have him brought in." Erika signed the clipboard he offered and watched until he reached for the phone. She felt a rush of elation as she made her way across the hall. Inside, she closed the door, and rested against it with closed eyes. It was several seconds before she could walk to the table and sit down. She was being silly, yet the prospect of talking to someone who had known Rick in the last two years excited her. She'd planned to leave if the sergeant outside said Kimball wasn't allowed visitors, but he hadn't, and she was here.

Erika was totally unprepared for Ty Kimball. She had read he was nineteen, but he looked fifteen. With a painfully thin body and watery blue eyes, he was a pathetic sight. But more than that, Erika was struck by his placid expression. Most prisoners she interviewed were defiant, and it was apparent in their eyes and faces. Kimball looked almost serene.

She waited until his escort went outside before she spoke. "Sit down, Ty. I'm Erika Wheatly, Rick's sister."

His eyes roamed the room, carefully avoiding her face, before he sat. "I thought they said you're from the DA's office. I guess I didn't hear right." He seemed to take it for granted that he was wrong, and for the moment his mistake suited her fine. He reached in his shirt pocket and stopped. "Got a cigarette?" he asked.

"No, I don't. Sorry."

He pulled one from his pocket and lit it. "This is my last one," he said wistfully. "I just thought maybe I'd bum one from you." He turned his attention to the smoke rising in the air, watching it intently.

It was difficult for her to deal with his detachment. "Did you hear me, Ty? Rick Wheatly was my brother."

His head slumped to his chest. "I heard. I just don't know what to say." Seconds passed before he looked up at her. "Rick was my friend, and I'm sorry he's dead." He pulled on his cigarette. "See, I'm not too smart, and he took care of me and helped me." He shook his head. "Nobody took as good care of me as he did."

His simple eulogy touched her. "You miss him, don't you?" she said. He nodded slowly. "I miss him too." Her mind searched for a way to reach this boy. "Can you tell me about my brother?"

"Depends on what you want to know."

"How long were you together?"

"Six months, maybe a little longer. I don't know. We met in Texas and worked on a ranch together."

At last, Erika thought, they were finally getting somewhere. "Do you remember where in Texas, or the name of the man you worked for?"

Ty thought for a moment. "The ranch didn't have no towns close, but I remember we called our boss Hank."

Erika smiled. Her line of questions was getting her nowhere and she struggled not to show her impatience. "Did Rick ever mention me?"

"Yeah. He told me once you were going to be a lady lawyer. Was that true?"

"Yes. I was in law school when he left."

Ty smiled and almost laughed. "Ain't that somethin'! I know Rick never lied to me, but I thought sometimes he joshed me."

She was sorry when her words rolled out edged with restlessness. "Ty, I don't have much time. If I ask you some questions, will you try to remember and answer them honestly?"

He nodded. "Yes ma'am."

"Did Rick tell you why he ran away from home?"

Ty tapped the ash from his cigarette into a small metal ashtray on the table. "He was afraid. I remember he told me he was afraid to stay in Denver."

Erika's eyes narrowed and she watched him closely. "Why was he afraid?"

"He was afraid of some man. He called him a name, but it was a funny name, and I don't remember it."

"But if you came to Denver, Rick wasn't afraid anymore, was he?"

"Yes ma'am, he was scared all right, but he was tired of being away from home and living like we was. Whatever was wrong, he wanted to come back and get it settled."

"How long were you here before he was shot?"

"A couple of days." Ty began to stammer and his words were jumbled. He stopped and drew in a long breath. "Rick didn't have no gun. I know he didn't. I never saw him with a gun as long as I knowed him."

Erika's heart jumped and she couldn't hide her shock. "Are you sure?"

"Why does everybody ask me if I'm sure? Rick didn't have no gun. I know it."

"Tell me about that night, Ty. Tell me everything you remember."

He rubbed his hands together and sighed. "They had no call

to kill him. We weren't robbin' no store. We went through the roof just to have a warm place for the rest of the night. Them old run-down buildings where we stayed before were cold and had rats in 'em. When the cops come, we run out the front door. We were both scared. Rick told me to run. I was around the corner headin' for the back when I heard the shots.''

"Then you didn't see him when he was shot?" He shook his head. "How many shots were fired?"

He dropped his eyes. "I don't know. It was two, maybe three. I was too scared to count."

"Have you told the police what you told me?"

"Yeah, but they don't believe me. They think Rick shot at a cop and he couldn't. He didn't have no gun."

"What happened after you were caught?"

He sat up straight. "I wasn't caught. When I heard the shots, I threw my hands in the air and stopped. I didn't want to get shot. I gave up. I don't want nothin' to do with guns."

Erika hated to undermine his pride. "You were very wise," she said. "What happened after you gave up?"

"The cop that chased me put the cuffs on me and we went back to the front of the store. Rick was down in the street, and the other cop was roaring around swearing and acting crazy braggin' about gettin' him. Rick laid there bleeding. He never said nothin'. Them cops called for an ambulance and we waited." Ty reached in his shirt pocket and pulled out an empty cigarette package. He crumbled it with his fingers and threw it in the ashtray. "It was all my fault. I was the one who found the way into the store because I was cold."

No wonder the grand jury. Ty interrupted her thoughts. He'd asked a question and she hadn't heard. "I'm sorry," she mused. "What did you say?"

"Rick's girl. Does she know he's dead?"

"What girl?"

"You know. Janey. He went to see her the very day we got here. I didn't want him to leave me because I was scared, but he went anyway."

Erika searched her memory. If Rick went to see a girl on his first day back in Denver, she had to be someone he had known before he left. Ty lapsed into silence and stared at the floor. Inside her head, flashes of a dark-haired girl with huge round eyes kept occurring. "What was Janey's last name, Ty?"

"Don't know," he answered. "Rick just called her Janey."

It was important for her to remember Janey, but it wasn't likely she'd do it here. She left her chair and called to him as she went out of the room. "I'll be right back." When she returned, the officer at the door inspected the packages of cigarettes and candy bars she'd purchased from the vending machines downstairs.

In the long run, she would be able to see Ty again, but if Renquist found out about her visit today, it might be a while. She gave him the gifts and left. On the way to her office, as she concentrated on driving, the name Janey Langley popped into her head.

# *Chapter Seven*

---

ERIKA MET ALICE just before noon at a downtown cafeteria. With the exception of a few questions, Alice listened to Erika for over twenty minutes while she related a short version of her morning activities. Alice swallowed and placed her fork on her plate. She shook her head and looked at her friend. "Let me get this straight. You want me to find Janey Langley for you. Am I right?"

Erika pulled her chair closer to the table. "That's right. It shouldn't be too difficult. I'm certain she went to the same school as Rick."

Alice spoke with some impatience. "I know it won't be difficult, if she's still in town. I'm wondering if it's the right action to take."

"Don't you see, Alice? Rick went to see her as soon as he got to Denver. He must have trusted her more than he did me. She talked to him, and I want to know where he was, maybe . . ." She paused, thinking she'd been a wretched sister, ". . . and maybe she knows why he ran away." Erika stared at the untouched salad on her plate. "I was so wrapped up in school and losing my parents, I wasn't much of a sister, or I'd know more about Janey and his other friends."

Alice sipped her tea thoughtfully. "What if she tells you things about Rick you don't want to know? Perhaps it's better to leave it alone. You can't change what happened and you might not be prepared for what she'll say."

Erika gripped her hands in her lap. Alice had a point she'd be wise to consider. She assumed whatever she discovered would make her feel better, and it might not be so. She tried to hide her annoyance as color rose in her cheeks. Shaking her head, she insisted, "I want to talk to Janey, even if she tells me things I don't want to hear."

Alice finished her food and settled back in her chair. "Why did you choose me to find her for you?"

"Because you're my best friend and you'll be discreet. I really don't believe she had anything to do with Rick's death, but just in case Ty Kimball mentions her, I don't want anyone to scare her off. I want to talk to her first." Erika looked down. "Renquist's issued a memo forbidding anyone in our office to talk to me about the hearing. I could find her, but it would be inconvenient, considering." She stopped, making a gesture of disgust. "Getting to Janey first is important to me."

Alice frowned. "It may already be too late."

"You may be right," Erika allowed, "but I have to try."

"And what about Kimball?" Alice questioned.

"He's iffy. He remembered Janey like an afterthought. He may never think of her again. Who knows?" Erika hung her head and shook it. "He told me he wasn't too smart, and he's right. He's a scared, sad young man, and if I had my own law practice, I'd be inclined to defend him myself. I'm that certain he told the truth."

Alice warned, "You could be completely wrong about him."

"Possibly, but I don't think so."

Alice glanced obliquely at Erika's food. "You haven't touched it. Eat. You don't want to lose that luscious figure."

"I'll try, but I'm not hungry." She knew Alice was considering her request, and she hoped for a positive answer, but she wasn't getting it.

"Don't try. Do it," Alice commanded. With a touch of wariness, she asked Erika, "How do you feel about the grand jury and Josh?"

Erika made a face and forced down a bite of salad. "After talking with Ty, it's obvious why it's being held. Ty was so positive Rick didn't have a gun, and since one was found near him . . ." Erika began to nibble again and stopped. "Mitch thinks the investigation is just a political ploy to get the city dads and the press off the department's back. He thinks Josh is the fall guy, that's why he's defending him."

"My God! Josh retained Mitch?" Erika smiled slightly and nodded. "How could Mitch do this to you?"

"I understand his reasons. I just told you why he accepted Josh's case."

"You understand his reasons. That's really funny. Tell Mitch Logan to let someone else defend Josh before it causes problems between you. You don't need any more trouble." Erika attempted to come to Mitch's defense, but Alice waved her off. "I don't care if he's right. Mitch doesn't need the publicity or the money, and there are dozens of good attorneys who could defend Josh. Tell him to back away from this one."

Alice always gave advice freely, and Erika knew, no matter what she replied, her friend would have an argument to counteract her answer. She had an awful feeling she should've asked Mitch to decline, but how sensible it seemed Friday to let him have his way. "If I know Mitch, it's too late for him to back away. If it makes you feel better, I wish I'd persuaded him not to represent Josh, but I didn't."

"Give it another try, Erika. Talk with him. I'm sure he'll understand."

She wished she were as confident as Alice. "I'll think about it," Erika said.

Alice was circumspect. "How about you and me?"

"What about us?"

"I have to warn you, Erika. You shouldn't get mixed up in this." Alice bent over the table. "You were indiscreet seeing Kimball this morning without his lawyer's permission. Since you told me, we could both be in trouble." Erika slumped and stared at her. "You aren't thinking clearly. Kimball probably was assigned an attorney from my office."

"I know that but . . ."

"Give it up and stay out of it completely. It's not like you to be reckless, and I can't believe you've included me in your folly."

Erika asked weakly, "Are you going to report me?"

"Not me, but we need to understand each other. The only conversation we had today was woman talk." Alice fussed around in her chair nervously. "And I can't help you find Janey. Sorry but . . ."

Erika interrupted. "I hoped you'd say yes."

"I can't . . ."

Erika considered what she'd done to her friend. It was a long moment before she spoke. "Sorry, Alice. I didn't think. I'm so accustomed to telling you everything. I placed you in a position . . ." Sad-faced, she stopped. "Don't get into trouble because of me."

"There isn't going to be any trouble," Alice assured her. "I don't know anything about your visit to juve this morning, okay?"

"Okay, since I didn't tell you, you can't possibly know."

Alice searched her face, then regarded her sternly. "You're not going to take my advice and stay out of this, are you?"

"Janey Langley is my only connection to Rick. Don't ask me to ignore her. She may be the only person who knows why he ran away."

Alice's face was dour. "I don't approve, Erika, but I wish you luck."

Erika swallowed hard. "Thanks for not telling me I'll need it."

"You will," Alice added.

Back at the office, Erika found the work Rhonda provided and a note. Mitch called at ten, leaving the message he'd see her later in the evening. Throwing herself into the task of finding Janey occupied her. Two hours later, she contacted her. They set up a meeting at Buckingham Square near the Orange Julius stand at six o'clock.

Mitch didn't call again before she left to make her appointment. She wanted to see him to ask him not to defend Josh. Alice was right, she couldn't bear a quarrel with him now; and another separation, perhaps a permanent one, was unthinkable.

When a small, dark young lady approached the bench where Erika sat and said, "Hi, Miss Wheatly," Erika remembered her instantly. "Hi, Janey," she replied. "It's nice of you to see me. I need to talk with you. Would you care for something to drink?"

"No, thanks," Janey said breathlessly and sat down beside her. "I'm on a break from the shoe store and I can't talk too long."

Erika studied her. "You've grown up, Janey. You're a young woman now."

Janey blushed. "I'm almost nineteen."

Their simple beginning made Erika feel strange. A prickle of fear darted down her spine and her arms grew cold. She hesitated before she spoke. "Janey, I know you talked to Rick before he died."

Erika saw her beam. "He came to see you then. I'm glad he decided to. I know he wanted to see you."

A combination of joy and regret filled Erika. "Rick didn't come to see me. He came back to town with a boy, Ty Kimball. He told me Rick went to see you." She watched closely, but couldn't see any change on Janey's face. "You talked to Rick. What was he doing the last two years? How did he manage? You know, I never knew why he ran away. Can you tell me anything?"

"Not much about where he was after he left. He didn't say much about it, but . . ."

"But what?"

"Before he left, he made me promise I'd never tell anyone why he ran away, and I haven't." She became ill at ease and would not meet Erika's eyes. "I know he didn't want you to know about it. He was so ashamed."

"It can't matter to him now. Please tell me. You can't imagine how important it is to me. I've wondered so many times what I did or didn't do to cause him to leave."

"It wasn't your fault. I can tell you that much." Janey's voice betrayed her distress. "He didn't want you to know what he'd done."

"Know what?" Erika persisted.

"Oh, Miss Wheatly, it started out as one of those dumb high school initiations and it got complicated and . . ." She stopped and cleared her throat. "I really don't know why he did what he did. It started out innocently enough and it just grew and grew."

Erika heard the hopelessness in her voice and she began to feel she'd get nothing from this girl. "Please, Janey?"

"I don't know how to begin."

"Tell me why he was ashamed."

"There was a group of kids who stole things and sold them for extra money. They all knew it was wrong, but if they wanted to join the Jocks they had to do it at least once. Somehow Rick got mixed up with them, just like a lot of other kids. That's what he was doing." Tears came to her eyes. "And wouldn't you know the groups in our school broke up after he ran away and wasn't there to help them anymore."

Erika's throat grew tight and the large lump settling there hurt. "Oh." Her voice failed and she had to wait a few seconds for it to return. "Rick was afraid I'd find out?"

Janey twisted her hands together. "That's part of it, but he was mostly afraid of some man."

"What man? Who was he?"

"The one who helped them sell the things they stole."

Dismayed at the turn in the conversation, Erika attempted to clear her mind. "You're telling me my brother was a thief . . ."

"Rick didn't steal," Janey interrupted indignantly. "He didn't have anything to do with any robberies or shoplifting." There was a certain amount of pride in her words. "He was the manager and kept track of the money, and stuff like that.''

Erika raised her voice deliberately. "Do you know what you're saying? You're telling me Rick managed a gang of thieves and a man helped him run it?''

Janey's dark eyes grew darker, then clouded over. "That's about it,'' she choked.

Erika's hands were shaking. "Explain this to me. For some reason, I can't comprehend what you're telling me.''

"The man, he helped them. He would call if some store left their door open, or if a place was easy to get into, then he helped them sell the stuff. Even with the money they shared with him, Rick's group was ahead of the other one. Both groups were doing the same thing, but Rick's sorta had extra help.''

Janey looked surprised at Erika's automatic moan of disgust. "All of this over a stupid contest. I can't believe it." Each word she heard filled her with more frustration. "I can't believe it,'' she repeated in a whisper.

Janey spoke more cautiously. "You haven't heard it all, and since I've gone this far, I might as well tell you the rest. The night Rick left town, the man and he got careless and unloaded some stolen merchandise in a buyer's truck. They didn't know a bum was sleeping behind a dumpster in the alley. He saw and heard everything. Rick ran, but that creep stayed and beat the old man over the head. Rick was sure he was dead, and he was certain the man saw him watching. Rick was scared he would be killed because of what he saw.''

Erika mustered her waning courage. "Did anyone else witness the murder?'' Janey shook her head. "Why didn't you tell someone, Janey?''

She received a flat answer. "And who would you tell, the police? Confess you'd been breaking the law?''

"I wish either you or Rick had told me.'' They sat without speaking for several long moments. Some way Erika knew the answer before she asked the question, "Do you know this man's name?''

"No, Rick called him a stupid name." Janey appeared to be thinking. "Renegade Rat, that's it. Rick called him Renegade Rat."

The name brought a sad smile. That was her brother, for sure. He nicknamed everyone. "And I suppose you've forgotten the names of the gang members?" Erika spoke caustically and she was sorry, but before she could apologize, Janey answered.

"You don't understand. I didn't see anything or do anything. Everything I know, Rick told me. I don't want any trouble. I just want to work at my job and get enough money to go to college." Janey began to sound as if she were apologizing. "I was crazy about your brother. I'd have done anything he asked. I wanted to run away with him, but he wouldn't hear of it."

Erika saw Janey check her watch. She took her hand and held it tight. "One more question and I'll go. Did Rick mention me when you talked?"

"Miss Wheatly, he came back because he was tired of running. He wanted to come home; being away wasn't easy for him. He didn't want to contact you until he knew it was safe for him to return." Janey lowered her head. "He was afraid for his life, and he was sorry for what he'd done. You have to believe that."

Salty tears stung Erika's eyes. She patted the small hand she still held. "Thanks. It means a great deal to me to know he wanted to come home."

"He loved you, Miss Wheatly, so don't think bad things about him. All of us do dumb things sometimes."

Appalled and bewildered, Erika forced a quiet tone. "May I call you again? Perhaps we could have lunch and talk more about Rick."

Janey smiled. "Sure," she said, "I'd like to."

Erika walked away quickly, thinking her brother, like so many people, didn't know when to quit. With lips pushed tightly together and tears threatening to tumble from her eyes, Erika ran from the shopping mall. She sat in her car for a long time. She couldn't excuse Rick; his behavior was morally and legally wrong. Yet, if only he'd come to her, they might have worked it out together, and the ending would've been happier. Behind all her thoughts a vengeful nagging lurked. Somewhere out there, someone went on his daily routine, and she wanted his scalp.

At home, she prepared a plate of sandwiches and opened a bottle of wine. She blocked out the events of the day, thinking only of Mitch. He would come and make the day's accumulation of pain go away. She changed her clothes and was combing her hair when he arrived.

She experienced a glow of excitement when he appeared dressed in a spiffy brown business suit and tie. He always looked assured and handsome. There was no spoken greeting; he swooped her in his arms and kissed her. This was what she waited for, and she returned his kiss eagerly. When he released her, he smiled at her. "You really know how a man likes to be welcomed."

"What did you expect?" she asked, still clinging to him.

"Just what I got." He kissed her again. She pulled back and straightened her hair as Mitch looked at her thoughtfully.

"Come sit down," she offered. "Do you mind if we don't go out?"

Mitch grinned expectantly. "Your invitation intrigues me. I'd love to stay here with you." He pulled her to the couch. "I could stay here with you forever."

Erika laughed uneasily. "I made sandwiches. Are you hungry?"

He reached for her. "Not for sandwiches," he murmured as his arms slipped around her waist.

Wiggling free of him, she told him in a slightly husky voice, "We need to talk." She glanced at his face and her resolve began to fade. "It's important," she urged.

His eyes mocked her. "I wonder how often passion is squelched by talk? There's too much talk."

"You're teasing me?"

"A little," he chuckled. His smile stimulated a wave of desire and it exhilarated her. He was too close and his scent and body intoxicated her.

"Stop it, Mitch."

"Stop what?" he drawled.

She turned her back to him. "You know."

"You win," he groaned. "We talk first." She plopped down beside him and his hand tousled her hair. "Let's have it. What's bothering you?"

"I'm worried about us and . . ."

He read her mind again. "And the hearing?"

She pulled her legs beneath her and settled down. "Yes. It frightens me," she admitted.

"Nonsense. A hearing can't hurt you."

She swept his objection aside. "Yesterday, we struck a tacit bargain, and today, I question whether or not I can keep my part of the agreement. Won't you find another lawyer for Josh? It'd make me feel so much better. I don't want you to be involved in this."

"Damn," he shouted, bringing his fist down hard in his left hand. Erika was not surprised at his reaction. "I tried to get you to tell me how you felt yesterday. Why didn't you tell me then?"

"I did, in a way. I told you I wanted to run from all this, but you ignored me." She drew in a breath and began speaking louder and faster. "Doesn't it occur to you your self-assurance, reputation and experience intimidate me? When you're near, it's almost impossible for me to say no to you."

"Like hell it is," he said with a comic weariness. His mouth twitched and she looked away. "Look at me, Erika." She obeyed instinctively. "It's too late. Manning and I spent the entire afternoon preparing. How can I get out of it now?"

Even in the face of defeat, she refused to give up. "Call Josh and tell him you changed your mind. It isn't hard to do. Please, call him."

"And what about my word? I gave the man my word and I don't like to break it. You may take it lightly, but I don't."

"I know you don't, and I admire that, but it can't hurt your reputation just this once. Do it because of us."

He continued to justify his actions. "You said Manning deserved a good defense." His eyes raked her face with cruel determination.

She stood her ground, holding her own. "And Rick was my brother. Josh killed him. Right or wrong, he shot and killed Rick. And that fact doesn't exactly endear Josh to me."

Mitch raised his voice in heat. "Your brother was robbing a drugstore, he committed a criminal act. Should a good police officer be sacrificed for a common . . ." He stopped abruptly, refusing to let the last word slip from his mouth.

Erika bristled with pain and anger. "For a common criminal?" She stiffened and jerked away from his hand seeking hers.

He walked away from where they sat. "Apologies are always flat, Erika, but I owe you one. I'm sorry."

She sounded quiet and deadly. "At least, I know how you feel." Her nose wrinkled in distaste. "You'll do as you please no matter what I say." She couldn't stop the sarcastic words, "You don't know what it's like to be wrong, do you?"

'My remark was a perfectly rotten jab, best left in the courtroom where it belongs. Please forgive me. Passing judgment is not my style, and I was wrong. You have every right to be angry."

"I don't need your permission to be angry. It comes easily," she quipped.

"Erika," he pleaded as he turned to look at her, but she stopped him short.

"Stop it, Mitch. I don't have to be hit with a baseball bat to get the message. Defending Josh means more to you than I do.''

He rushed toward her. ''You're wrong.''

She held up her hand to restrain him. ''Spare me your logic. I don't feel logical.'' She slumped down not looking at him. Ice hung in the air. ''We have nothing further to discuss. Don't you think you should go?'' She felt the divan sink under his weight.

''No,'' he said bluntly.

Erika told herself he was an unreasonable man and she was out of her mind to love him. She shuddered. Admitting she loved Mitch prompted her to groan aloud. What a time to acknowledge her true feelings, in the middle of a fight. She didn't dare think this way. They had no understanding; no pledges of any kind existed between them. It made her angry to be second on his list of priorities, but she'd never been number one. Assuming she was first was her mistake. His profession was number one.

The sound of his voice drew her back to reality. ''I don't understand what the hassle is about,'' he was saying. ''We went over this yesterday. What changed your mind, Erika?''

She raised her head and her eyes riveted to his. ''A pathetic young man named Ty Kimball.'' His eyes narrowed to thin slits. ''He told me Rick didn't have a gun, and heaven help me, I believe him.'' Mitch started to say something and she stopped him. ''No more arguments, I want you to listen. It's possible, maybe more than a seed of doubt, that Josh lied about Rick having a gun.'' He attempted to interrupt, but she would have none of it. ''Listen to me. It may be far out, but if, for some reason, Josh killed my brother deliberately, and you got him off, I would never forgive you. What if Josh meant to kill him? He wouldn't admit it.''

''That's dumb! Why would he admit to killing Rick when he didn't do it? You said he didn't know Rick.''

''Josh's story doesn't jibe; it sounds fishy.''

Mitch looked away, a half-uncertain laugh escaped him. "You don't know his story, and we're fighting over nothing. Manning is innocent." He slapped his hands on his knees and started to get up. Erika pulled him back.

"You must know something you won't or can't discuss with me."

His eyes grew narrow. "And you know more than you're telling me."

"Josh could be lying."

"Nonsense! The case is cut and dried. No problem. Trust me."

"Be sure, Mitch. Be absolutely certain. I mean what I say. Any good lawyer can represent him, if the case is cut and dried as you say. Why waste your time?"

Mitch ventured a smile. "You make a powerful point, lady. I bet you're a tiger in the courtroom."

"Well, finally," she said in relief. "You'll tell Josh tomorrow you can't defend him?"

"Erika, I thought you knew. The hearing begins tomorrow."

She almost wailed. "So soon?"

"The DA put it on an early calendar. I suspect he did because of your connection with his office, and Josh is anxious to have it over, so we didn't object. That's why I spent most of the day with him."

Erika bit her lip. What else could go wrong? "I had no idea it would start this soon."

"Well it is, and to me, the early date is just one more indication of the political nature of the whole show."

She sighed. "Promise me, if the investigation turns sour and charges are brought against Josh, you won't defend him during his trial. I'll settle for that."

Mitch winced. "Withdraw from my client? That would be harmful to both Josh and to me. You know that. Besides, it would be unprofessional." He stopped and smiled, admiration lighting his eyes. "You try to cover all bases, don't you? Very good strategy. He stroked her cheek. "Josh won't be charged and there won't be a trial. I know."

"Promise me," she insisted.

He shook his head. "Why? I just told you there won't be a trial."

Her voice was rising, yet she continued to insist. "Will you promise me?"

Her dogged approach irritated him. His voice, too, rose. "Don't treat me like a witness you're browbeating. I'm not on trial and a yes or no answer just won't hack it."

She couldn't understand his stubborn refusal to promise her. "You keep your word. All I want is your assurance if it comes to a trial, you won't defend Josh."

"If—if—if—your whole premise is based on *ifs*. All I want is for you to stay out of this, and since you talked to Ty Kimball, I'm certain you won't." He took her face in his hands and forced her to look at him. She lowered her eyes to defy him. "Stay out of it," he warned.

"You think Josh is a saint; you think Rick was a common criminal; you're always right, and I'm always wrong." She stopped to breathe and jerked away. "We have nothing more to discuss." She stood and pointed to the door. "This time I'm telling you to leave." Livid, she faced the coldest brown eyes she'd ever seen. Without a word or hesitation, he left, slamming the door behind him. Erika walked to the door and pounded it with her fists, giving in to her anger and frustration. He's as stubborn as he is obtuse, she told herself angrily. Remembering his unforgiving eyes, she stopped beating the door and began to tremble. Trying to believe she didn't care if she ever saw him again didn't work, and she went to the kitchen, wrapped the sandwiches in Saran wrap and put them in the refrigerator, then poured the wine back into the bottle.

The phone woke her at eleven. She answered it quickly, expecting it to be Mitch.

A frightened voice asked, "Miss Wheatly?"

"Yes."

"This is Janey Langley."

"What can I do for you, Janey?"

"I thought you should know. After you left this evening, a man came to the shoe store. He served me with a paper. I have to appear at a grand jury hearing tomorrow. It has something to do with Rick."

Caught unaware, Erika said, "Oh?"

"What should I do?"

Erika was astounded. "You have to go, Janey. Don't try to duck it. They can force you, if they need to, so don't run, whatever you do."

Janey sobbed, "Why did you tell them about me? I thought I could trust you. I didn't do anything, and now I'm all messed up. I wish I'd never talked to you."

"I didn't tell them about you, Janey. I haven't told anyone." She had told Alice, but Alice didn't have anything to do with this. She wavered. No, no, Alice wouldn't do this to her.

"Yes you did, so don't you call me anymore expecting me to tell you things about Rick, because I won't talk to you." Erika pulled the phone away from her ear when she heard the sharp click.

At two o'clock, Erika was still awake, wondering who found out about Janey. Ty could have said something to his attorney, she supposed, but who requested Janey's appearance before the grand jury? Renquist or Mitch? She felt cold when logic told her Dick Renquist must have made the request.

# Chapter Eight

IT WAS SHORTLY after eight in the morning when Erika appeared in Dick Renquist's office, at his call. Renquist looked up from his desk, glanced at her quickly, signed two more papers, then motioned with his head for her to sit down. Erika had entered his office smiling, but his greeting and the strained atmosphere in the room caused the smile to fade. She sat down, adjusted her skirt, and waited. He placed the pen in its holder on the desk and leaned back in his chair. His face was somber and he avoided looking directly at her. When he finally spoke, he sounded both irritated and sad. "Well, Erika, what do you have to say for yourself?"

The sinking feeling in her stomach was coupled with one of chagrin. Last night, she'd gone over what she'd say if this happened. Dick knew. Considering his attitude, it couldn't be more obvious. Yet faced with reality, not a rehearsal, her mind worked diligently trying to find a reasonable answer and failed. "I'm not a mind reader," she told him. "What do you mean?" What a silly response, she thought, resisting an urge to roll her eyes and shake her head.

He handed her the memo he issued during her absence. "Read this and don't tell me you didn't know about it. You knew yesterday before you went to see Ty Kimball." He glared at her with unwavering eyes.

Weakly, she rose to her own defense. "This memo was for the office personel. Rhonda told me about it, but I didn't read it."

"But you knew?"

Erika nodded. "You're keeping me in the dark about the investigation, and how my brother died. All I know is what I read in the papers. I have a right to know. Rick was my brother and my only relative. I want to know what happened and what's going on.''

Renquist pointed his finger at her. ''You, young lady, have no right to jeopardize this department's investigation, and you disobeyed a direct order from your superior. That's enough to put you on hold for a while.''

''There was no direct order. Your memo didn't say I couldn't see Kimball.'' She waved it under his nose. ''Show me where it says, Erika Wheatly is forbidden to visit the boy who was the last person to talk to her brother before he died.''

His eyes flared and his jaw set stubbornly. ''Don't nit-pick with me, and don't avoid the issue. You were to stay clear of this case and everyone involved in it, and you ignored the order.''

Erika continued to insist. ''I'm a relative and I have a right . . .''

He interrupted her rudely. ''Being a relative doesn't give you right one, and you know it.''

Erika wondered why she continued with this bluff, but she was angry now. Her eyes flashed. ''This office represents the people of Denver and whether I work here or not, I'm one of those people.'' She lowered her eyes. ''I have a right to know what's going on.'' Looking at him, she realized she'd made a mistake. Her insistence had alienated him completely.

He spoke deliberately. ''My memo was clear enough and you chose to ignore it. It's as simple as that, and I won't allow it. You've embarrassed me and the department.'' He threw a letter across the desk at her. ''Read this,'' he ordered. ''It was hand-delivered to me late yesterday afternoon. Keep it. The public defender's office was kind enough to send a copy for both of us.'' Her heart sank to her toes as soon as she began to read. ''You understand it don't you? The defense attorney for Kimball has filed charges against you.'' He paused for only a moment. ''They're serious charges, Erika.''

She looked at the signature. "Who's Jay Macomber? I don't know him."

"A sharp lawyer who has his wits about him. That's who." Renquist's voice seemed over-loud. "You questioned Kimball without his lawyer being present. The least you could have done was obtain his permission. Now, you and this office are in trouble." He rapped the desk with his fist. "That was stupid, Erika." He left his chair and began to pace. She knew men vented their frustration by pacing and Erika hoped it would also control his anger. After a few steps, he spoke thoughtfully. "I must decide what to do with you."

Erika had underestimated the diligence of Ty's attorney when she took a risk she thought minimal. The idea that Renquist might take serious disciplinary action hadn't occurred to her. A chewing-out was all she expected. She held her breath for a moment. His anger had disappeared, leaving her frightened. She liked the angry feeling better. "I just wanted to talk to Kimball and ask him about Rick. I wasn't gathering evidence for or against anyone."

"Then you shouldn't have told the guard you were from the DA's office. You tried to make it look like an official visit."

"How else could I get to see him?"

Renquist glared at her, but ignored her question. The anger from his face faded and he sounded gloomy. "I know you wanted to see Kimball more for personal reasons than professional ones. I know it," he repeated, "but now if we want to press the case against this young man, Macomber will ask to have it thrown out because of you."

Erika sighed heavily. "Answer a question for me. Does Kimball have a previous record?" She turned to see him shake his head. "Then it hardly matters. Breaking and entering is the only real charge you have. Nothing was taken. Considering it's his first offense, he'd get off with probation anyway. I don't believe I've destroyed the case against Kimball."

"You're a smart lawyer." Renquist stopped and corrected himself. "At least you were until this happened. But you aren't too sharp about politics. Your conduct with Kimball was less than professional, and the public defender's office loves this sort of thing. They eat it up. Forget about hurting the Kimball case. They're after your hide and mine. Getting you reflects on this office. That's their main intention. Our two offices are enemies, remember? Even if I fired you today, a reprimand or probation from the bar association will make the papers. This office is going to catch it whatever I do.''

She spun around to face him. ''The bar association!''

''The opposition has a legal right to insist you answer the charges in front of the association.''

Her anger returned. ''Everyone has rights but me,'' she barked.

Although there was a hint of sorrow in his tone, his words were harsh. ''You acted irrationally, Erika, and I'm afraid you'll have to answer for it.''

She twined her fingers in her hair and searched wildly for a way out of the dilemma. Unable to see one, she spoke with resignation. ''Tell me what you want me to do and I'll do it. It's my fault and I'll do what I can to right the wrong.''

Renquist walked back to his desk and sat down. His breath escaped his body slowly. ''You're not going to like this, but I have to do something. First, I'm going to suspend you without pay until the Kimball action and this grand jury business with Manning are over.'' He straightened his tie and warned her. ''Stay out of it, Erika, or I'll ask for your resignation.'' She opened her mouth to thank him for not firing her, but her vocabulary deserted her and she slumped in her chair. ''Second,'' he continued, ''you're to prepare a letter for Macomber explaining your actions and trying to convince him to withdraw his charges.'' He looked at her from under his eyelids. ''Make it good, Erika.'' A chill trailed down her spine. ''In addition, I'd get me a lawyer if I were you. Tell him everything and let him help you with the letter.'' His eyes narrowed and a furrow appeared on his brow. ''It's called being prepared. If you don't convince Macomber to drop his charges with a letter of apology, someone will have to represent you at the bar association hearing." He appeared self-conscious when he added, "Ask Mitch. He might do it, and he'd be a good choice. He has influence in this town and ample experience with these matters."

"Mitch is representing Josh. What about a conflict?"

He considered her question without surprise. "You might have a point. If he won't, he can recommend someone." Erika rose and walked to the door. For the first time, Dick spoke hopefully. "Go home and get to work on the letter. With some luck, maybe we can get this settled with as little damage as possible."

"Thanks, Dick, for not firing me on the spot. I appreciate the chance you're giving me."

"Scat," he snorted.

Visions of her name in banner headlines continued to plague her as she removed a few personal belongings from her desk and packed them in her briefcase. She could picture them now. ERIKA WHEATLY DISBARRED. Self-rebuke filled her. She had only herself to blame. It was ironic—one of the few times in her life she'd gambled, she'd lost. Alice was right to warn her. The more she assessed the situation, the more she was certain, she needed a good attorney. Swallowing her pride, she asked Rhonda to call Mitch's office and make an appointment for her. Her fingers drummed the desk as she waited. When Rhonda buzzed her and informed her she had a four-thirty appointment, she was both pleased and puzzled. How had Rhonda managed an appointment with *the* Mitchell Logan the same day she called? A sound from the hall reminded her she wanted to get out of this place without having to explain her departure too many times. Explaining to Mitch was going to be bad enough for one day. Erika closed her briefcase and looked around the office, then hurried from the room.

Erika took unusual care with her appearance for her appointment with Mitch. She was dressed in a soft, rose-colored suit, every blonde hair in place, and her makeup applied pains-takingly. She hoped no one would think she had a care in the world.

During the day, her emotions had been at war, but not now. What was done was done, and most important, she must keep her wits about her and cut her losses if possible. Even though she and Mitch argued too much, they weren't enemies. Then remembering his hasty exit from her apartment last night, she wasn't sure about that. But this was a legal matter. He'd un-derstand how awful it would be for her to lose her job. Or worse, forfeit her license to practice law. Erika squared her shoulders and opened the door.

In an outer office, a pleasant woman in her forties sat at a large desk listening on the phone. She smiled at Erika, ac-knowledging her presence. Returning the receiver cautiously with a light touch, she said, "You must be Erika Wheatly." Erika nodded. "Mr. Logan is on the phone. Why don't you sit down? I'm sure it won't be long before he's finished."

Erika thanked her and sank into a soft, comfortable oversized sofa. The outer door opened and a well-dressed blonde ap-proached the desk and spoke with the receptionist. A buzzer sounded and the woman at the desk leaned to the intercom. She turned to Erika. "Mr. Logan will be right out."

Almost immediately, he stood before her. "This is a pleasure and a surprise. I didn't expect to see you again so soon, Erika. Please come in." He guided her into his office and helped her into a chair at the left of his desk. He stood near her. "You haven't seen my office, have you?" He stretched out his arms. "What do you think?" he asked in an aloof and guarded manner. She recalled vividly how he stormed from her apart-ment, enraged. Today his behavior was polite but cautious.

She forced her attention to the room. There was no doubt about it. It was elegant—rich, but tasteful. Her eyes came to rest on him. "It's beautiful, Mitch."

His response was brief. "Thanks." He seated himself in the brown leather chair behind his desk and looked at her with admiration. "That color becomes you. You look radiant today."

"It's nice of you to say so, but I'm not feeling radiant." His eyebrows drew together and she continued, watching his expression. "I'm in trouble, Mitch. I need your expertise."

His stone face relaxed and he appeared amused. "Are you asking me what I think you are?"

"Will you be my attorney? I hope you say yes. It's very important to me." She quickly opened her purse and handed him the letter from Macomber.

He took the letter from her hand and tapped it on his desk as he gave her a guarded look. "Before I read this, I need to know if it has anything to do with the Manning case."

She lowered her eyes to her hands. "Indirectly," she answered, "but . . ."

Mitch stopped her. "I can help you after the hearing is ended. Will that be too late?" He pushed the letter to her side of the desk and smiled for the first time. "You surprise me, Erika. I was prepared for a dozen questions from you about the grand jury today."

She returned the letter to her purse. He was being presumptuous and arrogant again. "I don't dare. I've been formally warned by Dick not to talk to anyone about it."

His smile grew warmer, but still cautious. "All the more reason to make you curious." He glanced at her face quickly. "Don't worry, Renquist wants a fair hearing and that's the way it should be. By the end of the week it will all be over and your office will be back to normal."

"Not for me, I'm afraid," she tried to keep her tone light, and failed. "I've been suspended, and the boss suggested I get a lawyer."

"You've what?" He stopped short and his businesslike expression gave way to one of curiosity.

"I've been suspended," she repeated as she stood and prepared to leave. "I was wrong to come here. I'll find someone else."

"Sit down." He spoke quietly, but nevertheless, it was a

command and she returned to the chair. "What did you do?"

She fumbled for the letter in her purse and threw it on his desk. "Read this and find out. It tells it all quite succinctly." Not wanting to anticipate his reaction, she stared down at the floor. She looked up at him when she thought he moaned. From the twinkle in his eyes, she knew he didn't moan, he laughed. "What's so funny?" she asked with some irritation.

"The threat of charges before the bar." He tossed the letter on the desk and put the palms of his hands together, resting his fingertips near his mouth. "I was remembering the first time an ambulance-chasing barrister brought me before the association." He laughed. "I slaughtered him."

It was difficult for her to hide her astonishment. "You've had charges brought against you?"

"Twice, as a matter of fact. And as you can see, it's not the end of the world."

"You've survived, but I'm not you. I'm afraid."

"So was I the first time." He folded his hands on the desk in front of him. "You mentioned Kimball last night, but I had no idea you went to see him without his attorney being present." He grinned. "And without Macomber's or Renquist's permission? Tsk, tsk, Erika."

"Stop teasing. This is serious."

"Yes ma'am," he drawled and corrected his slump in his chair.

"Don't do that," she ordered. "Just tell me you'll help me."

He continued in his best western drawl. "What would you like me to do, ma'am?"

She gritted her teeth. "Renquist wants me to draft a letter, to convince Macomber to back off. I need your help with the letter." She stopped, cleared the thickness from her throat, and looked into his amused face. "If the letter doesn't convince Macomber, I'll need you to defend me with the review board."

He thought for a few seconds. "It really was crummy timing

on your part. If you'd waited just a few days, no one would care if you talked to Kimball. You should have stayed out of it, Erika. That independent streak of yours causes you a lot of pain.''

She tossed her head. ''You just can't resist taking a jab at me, can you? I know I acted on impulse—without thinking it through. Now I'm sorry. Help me instead of blaming me. I won't act hastily again. You can count on it.''

''I hope so,'' he stated firmly. ''And I hope whatever information you gained from Kimball was worth what it may cost you.''

She answered meekly. ''Some of it was and some of it wasn't.'' His manner seemed detached, as if he were thinking about something else, then he began to write on a note pad.

''That's usually the way it is,'' he said and finished writing. He pressed the intercom. ''Mrs. O'Brien, will you come in please?'' He turned to Erika. ''I have some information to help you get started with the letter. Mrs. O'Brien will help you find it in my library. I have a meeting until nine. May I come to see you then and we'll finish our discussion?''

The secretary entered the room as Erika spoke. ''You'll help me then?''

Mitch's smile worked his magic on her again. She felt the flush, the weak knees, and she knew if she spoke, she would sound breathless and hoarse. ''Of course,'' he said. ''Was there any doubt?''

At home, Erika changed her clothes, found paper and pen, spread out the material she had brought from Mitch's office and began to work. Two of the articles dealt with a recent move on the part of some judges to require felons to make restitution to their victims in some form. A treatise on the rights of the accused didn't reveal anything new, but it was Mitch's way of reminding her of her duty. At least she guessed that's why he included it. This bothered her some, but she didn't have time to dwell on it. The interesting material was on the rights of families of victims of crime. As she read, her admiration for

Mitch's attention to detail grew. She'd done one thing right the last few days, choosing her attorney.

With the information she gathered from reading, Erika began to make an outline of her letter. She worked steadily until she opened the door to admit Mitch.

"Help me," he said as he juggled two large, flat boxes and two white cartons.

She relieved him of part of his burden and stepped aside. "What's this?"

Mitch headed for the kitchen. "Pizza and salad. I bet you didn't eat dinner and I know I haven't." He took off his jacket, tossed it over a chair and sat down. "Hurry, girl. Let's eat this before it gets cold." He opened the salad cartons. "Don't go to any bother. All we need are two forks and two napkins."

She found the items he requested and returned to the table. Eying the large amount of food he'd brought, she teased, "Half of this would be enough."

"I doubt it, I'm starved. Sit down." He pulled two slices of pizza away from the rest, placed one on her napkin and began to eat the other. He chewed, swallowed and sighed with pleasure. "Oh, that's good," he mumbled. "You haven't tasted yours. Try some, it's very good."

Erika ate and wondered why she found him so attractive. His strongly defined features were imposing and sensual, but there was more to this man than compelling looks. Tonight, she needed to keep their relationship professional, but his nearness always overpowered logic, and this was no exception. She wished she could stop thinking how wonderful he was. Remembering last night, she admitted he wasn't always kind or helpful. After taking a few more bites, she spoke. "Would you like something to drink?"

"How about some milk?"

Erika took the carton from the refrigerator and placed it on the counter. She poured two glasses, feeling his eyes on her as she fussed about. "You look great," he said as she placed the milk before him.

Back at the counter, she looked down at her jeans and shirt.

"You're being kind to me again," she remarked.

"I'm not. You look cute in jeans."

She rummaged in the cabinet for the coffee maker. Cute? No one had called her cute since she was in grade school. What's cute? Just another word to avoid a better description. What happened to sexy, appealing, even glamorous? Well, after the blowout last night, maybe she should settle for cute. "Yuck," she complained under her breath. She found the Mr. Coffee machine and placed it on the counter. "I read all the material you gave me today and started an outline for my letter. When do you think it should be mailed?"

He shook his head and swallowed hard. "You don't mail it. You take it to Macomber and you hand it to him personally. That is, if he'll see you. If he's not in, leave it with his secretary with instructions he's to read it immediately. But before you do anything, bring the final draft to my office and one of the typists will transcribe it onto my office stationery."

"That doesn't give us much time."

"We don't need much time. There are only a few things you can say which are relevant or may be effective, and you want to get in there quickly before Macomber has too long to fret about it." He finished his salad and helped himself to more pizza. "Have you met Macomber?" he asked.

"No, I haven't had the dubious pleasure."

He thought for a while. "I wonder how old he is."

"I have no idea."

"No matter. When you do meet him, look your prettiest and be your charming self. A few feminine wiles won't hurt your case. That is, if they're subtle." His lips curled upward at the corners. "Charm, Erika. Meet him with charm and confidence."

"Mitch Logan, are you suggesting because I'm a woman, I might get him to drop the charges?"

"Whatever works," he answered. Mitch feigned a frown and teased her. "Whatever is legal." He followed with an exaggerated wink.

"Mitch!"

"Don't pull that innocent act with me. All women know men are suckers for a pretty face and a shapely leg, and you have both. I know you didn't get through law school because you're beautiful, but it didn't hurt you." He smiled innocently. "More pizza?" She shook her head. "Then get me your draft and I'll look at it while I finish."

Erika was only slightly amused at his remarks as she found her notes in the living room. She reminded herself tonight there'd be no arguments. Mitch took the papers from her and began to read. She sat down and watched him, but from his expression, couldn't tell whether he liked it or not. He finished his milk, pulled a pencil from his coat and began circling things. "I like what I'm marking. Your notes reflect serious thought and that's good." He continued to read before he spoke again. She watched anxiously. "You cited the best precedents and mentioned the punishment Renquist imposed." He turned the paper to the back. "I want you to add these ideas. Own up to what you did. Show no fear and admit your mistake. Be honest about the reasons for your error. They may have fallen short of legal ethics, but they're valid. Then, in a contrite manner, make a pledge not to be reckless again. After all, the chances of your getting so emotionally involved due to a family relationship are nil." Finished, he handed the papers back to her. "I like it. You did very well." He looked at her quizzically. "You proved an old theory of mine wrong. I always believed lawyers made bad clients, but in this case it's the reverse. I admit I'm surprised."

She blushed faintly, proud of the compliment. "I'm glad you like it. Praise from you makes a suspended deputy DA feel better." It was important to her to earn his praise, and how good it was to hear. "I can't believe that's all," she said, not trying to hide her pleased smile.

He pushed back from the table. "That's it. Keep it as simple and short as possible, and don't forget to bring it to my office to be typed."

"Don't you want to see the final copy before I deliver it?"

"No, not after seeing the work you've done. I have confidence you'll do the job well."

She rode another wave of joy. "You're sure the letter is okay?"

He reached out and stroked her cheek. "Positive. Don't worry so. Even if Macomber can resist you and your letter, the bar association won't take your right to practice away." He paused and smiled reassuringly. "Well, not permanently," he added.

Erika breathed a sigh of relief. "You can't believe how happy it makes me to hear that. Thanks for your help, I truly appreciate it. With Rick, and now this, an end to all the madness can't come too soon."

"It will," he assured her cheerfully as he stood and stretched. "The coffee smells good. How about a cup, then I have to go. It's been a long day. After regular office hours, I met the movers. October is almost here, and it's time to get ready for the move to Vail."

She'd forgotten about the impending move. "Won't you miss your elegant office?" She went to the cabinet and chose her best cups and saucers for the coffee.

His eyes followed each of her movements. "I'm not sorry about moving to Vail. I'll enjoy being there more than I do Denver. It's just the mess and confusion. I'm an orderly person and that gets to me."

She volunteered. "I can help you. I don't have anything else to do now. Perhaps my help would take some pressure off. I'd be glad to do it, really."

"You're nice." He smiled at her. "But you'll be back to work before it's moving day."

"I don't know how. If I have to appear before the bar, it might take weeks. They're not noted for their speed."

His smile changed from warm to cagey. "With a prompting from me, they'll hurry."

She carried the coffee to the living room. Their hands touched as she handed him the cup and she felt more than excitement. Delicious anticipation would describe it better. She licked her lips. "Whether I'm working or not, let me help you move."

"We'll see," he replied.

She sat down on the couch, and he chose a chair across from her. He noted the time and sipped at his coffee. "Relax, Mitch, and enjoy the coffee. It's not late."

"There's work I have to do before the hearing tomorrow." He hadn't meant to mention the hearing. He hung his head in disgust, swearing quietly.

"Something unexpected happened?"

His discomfort intrigued her. "Yes, but there's nothing to worry about. I want to be prepared in any event. I don't like surprises in the courtroom."

Erika put her coffee cup down. "I wish we could talk about the case . . ."

"So do I."

She was beginning to suspect that in some way he regretted getting mixed up in it, and she wanted to know more. "Is Josh in trouble?" she ventured calmly.

He sounded agitated. "Not if he's told me the truth."

She patted the cushion next to her. "Sit here by me." He moved to the couch and placed his arm on the back of it, not around her. "What's wrong?" she whispered.

"Nothing. I have too much on my mind, I guess."

"Would it help if we stopped talking about the subject we shouldn't be discussing?"

"Maybe," he answered.

She wanted to tell him what Ty Kimball had told her, and share the information she learned from Janey. There was so much she longed to tell him and ask him. He was defending Josh Manning, the man who shot her brother, and he couldn't confide in her. Both were silenced by secrets they couldn't share. The finality of her sigh roused him.

"I should go. You're tired. It's been an upsetting time for you, and a busy one for me. There aren't enough hours in the day to accomplish what I need to do.''

Ever since the subject of Josh came up, Mitch had looked troubled, even if he tried to hide it. Erika longed to tell him everything and take her chances with the outcome, but luck wasn't exactly running in her favor. She suppressed the urge, resigning herself to do what was the most difficult for her, wait. ''You should go if you have work waiting for you. You want to be fresh for the hearing.''

''Are you throwing me out?''

She turned to look at him. ''Oh, no!''

''Well, you should,'' he said emphatically. ''Neither of us can say what we want to say.''

She dropped her head. ''I know. Will I see you tomorrow?'' she questioned, unable to control the urgency in her voice.

''We'll see,'' he replied. ''I'll call you. And Erika . . .'' Though he kept his face turned away, she had no trouble hearing him. ''I've changed my mind about a few things. Sorry, I've been a stubborn fool. When this mess is over, I hope you'll give me the chance to try to explain.''

After Mitch left, she worked on the letter, checking spelling, adding and deleting words and sentences. When she was convinced she'd caught everything, she reluctantly prepared for bed, afraid that sleep was hopeless. Mitch's parting words echoed in her thoughts until she finally fell asleep, sometime in the early hours of the morning.

# *Chapter Nine*

ERIKA HAD JUST opened the door and was kicking off her shoes when the phone rang. It was Mitch.

"How are you?"

"I'm fine," she said warmly.

"Mrs. O'Brien told me you came by the office and had the letter typed. How did it go? Did you see Macomber?"

Erika chuckled in a nervous manner. "For all the good it did me. I'm getting paranoid. I had visions of a fat old man sitting at a desk in his office, reveling in his power and refusing to see me. He wasn't like that at all."

He mumbled, "Oh?"

"No. We had a pleasant, civilized chat. He told me he'd let me know by Friday what he expects to do. At first, I was encouraged. Now, I'm not sure." She sighed. "I told you I'm paranoid."

"Maybe I can see him for you," he mumbled.

His offer brightened her day a little. "Oh, would you? I don't suppose there's any way you can find out the direction he's leaning, but I'd feel better if you tried."

There was another brief silence. Mitch was considering her request. Experience had taught her that she couldn't rush him. "We'll see, but I won't promise to do it today. I may postpone it until tomorrow."

She didn't like the way he sounded. He was remote, tired, maybe worried. If she could see him, she might know which. "You don't sound your usual self, Mitch. You sound tired or distracted."

He grunted. "I am. My mind's on the hearing. We're taking a well-needed break, but we'll be back at it soon." Erika said nothing, but from his preoccupation, she realized the hearing wasn't going the way he thought it should. Not daring to ask about the problem, Erika said, "I did what you told me this morning. I dressed in my best suit and I was *sooo* charming. I think you would've been proud of me."

He answered, "I'm sure I would."

She heard his fingers drumming on the side of the phone. "What's the noise?" It stopped immediately.

"Me." There was a moment's pause. This conversation is worse than last night's, she thought. And it's pointless to speculate on what had happened at the hearing to put him in such a funk. Still, she didn't want to lose the sound of his voice. "Tell me. Is there anything else I can do to help me out of the mess I made?"

His attention seemed to return. "You did all you could. Now, we wait." She heard another voice and waited through the silence. "Sorry, Erika, but I'm back in business. I have to go. Hang in there." He didn't say goodbye. The dial tone told her he was gone.

While she was at the phone, she called Alice, hoping to catch her for lunch, but she had left the office. The silence in the room seemed unnatural. She changed her clothes and walked briskly to the park, intending to meditate on her situation.

Of course, Mitch was her first problem. Admitting she loved him didn't change anything. He helped her, lent his support, attempted to make life easier for her. In fact, he did everything to indicate he loved her, everything except one important fact—he didn't say it. She mulled over the thought of telling him she loved him. Minutes passed while she considered his possible reactions to such a confession. He could say he loved her. He could say *adios*. He could propose she be his lover, not a wife. God, he could say or do so many things. Erika hated too many options. Knowing she couldn't make Mitch's choice for him, she continued to weigh the consequences of telling him how she felt. She paused, her legal training forcing her to examine her feelings rationally. There was only one fact. She loved Mitch whether he loved her or not. She kept coming back to how she felt about him. Perhaps it wasn't sane, but she loved what he did and how he looked. After all, she couldn't snuggle up at night with her job.

Quite unexpectedly, she thought of Rick and the money her parents left to him. It was hers now. With the money, a small law office was possible. She could even ditch everything in Denver and start over in another city. If she wanted, she could go back to school and teach law. Teaching would make it possible to stay in the business with none of the hassle. Maybe she would chuck it all for an island in the Pacific. She knew she wouldn't go to such extremes. Abandoning the law completely wouldn't suit her either. Yet, far-out thoughts of the island made her realize that she had more independence and many more options than she'd thought.

In any event, she couldn't just sit by passively. She had to do something. She decided she must tell him she loved him. The money could give her a way out if she needed it. Being conservative wasn't working for her—it was time to take a chance.

Completing a two-hour stroll, she returned home and called her parents' lawyer, making an appointment at one the next afternoon. One base was covered. What to do with the money depended on Mitch. That evening she scoured the paper for news of the hearing. One small, noncommittal article was all she found, and it produced no new information. She tossed the paper aside. It was usually crammed with events she could do without; when she wanted something, it wasn't there. At eleven, she gave up on Mitch and went to bed.

Alice called her early in the morning. After the greetings, she said, "I heard the news."

"What news?" Erika asked cheerfully.

"About that bum Renquist suspending you."

"News really gets around, doesn't it? How did you find out? Who told you?"

"I heard a rumor last night from Ted, so I called Rhonda this morning, and you know Rhonda." Alice heard Erika's laugh. "I must say you're taking it well. I didn't expect you would."

Brushing back her hair, Erika sat down. "The shock is over, and I know I'll survive."

"I hope you know I didn't have anything to do with it. I didn't tell."

"I never thought you did," she said. "There's a member of your organization named Macomber. He's Kimball's lawyer. He caught me."

Alice's voice lowered. "Macomber's not a bad guy. It could've been worse. You may have lucked out."

"That'll be the day," Erika remarked.

"It's good to know you don't blame me. I was a bit worried." A small pause passed. "Come have lunch with me. I have some fantastic news, and some office gossip to interest you."

Erika groaned. "You piqued my curiosity. Tell me the exciting news now. You know I hate to wait."

"Unh unh. This news must to be delivered in person. Meet me at Duffy's at one and I'll tell all."

"No, I can't make it at one. I have an appointment with my parents' lawyer. Rick had some money coming when he turned twenty-one. It's mine now."

"Drat," Alice exclaimed. "I won't be free until almost one. We need to talk, Erika. My news is important!"

Alice's usual serenity was missing. Something urgent sounded in her voice. "How about dinner?" Erika offered.

"Could we make it early?"

"Of course."

"Good. I'll meet you in front of the Broker at six. Okay?"

"Okay."

The rest of the day passed swiftly and it was no time before the two of them were seated in the vault of a former bank converted into a restaurant. The waiter offered them menus. Alice smiled broadly. "We want two of your best steaks, medium rare, baked potato with sour cream, and salad with blue cheese dressing." She stopped to catch her breath. "And wine, red wine. You choose it for us." Erika was speechless and she sat watching her wide-eyed and smiling friend. Alice turned to her happily. "My treat. Tonight we're celebrating."

She could tell Alice was almost beside herself with joy. Erika spoke through her laughter. "Somehow I thought we might be. Are you going to tell me why?"

"I'm dying to. I wanted to tell you first." Alice leaned across the table and grabbed her hands. "I'm going to be married. Ted asked me to marry him last night!"

Erika felt a rush of excitement. "Oh, Alice, I'm so happy for you." They laughed and squeezed each other's hands. Erika squelched a tug of jealousy. "Did you set the date?"

"Not a firm one, but we're thinking December. Maybe a Christmas wedding?" She looked away and took a tissue from her purse to wipe away happy tears. "I've been doing this off and on all day. I never understood women who cried when they were happy and look at me."

They waited quietly as the waiter poured the wine. Erika raised her glass. "Here's to your happiness, an entire lifetime of it." Their glasses clinked, and they drank. "What are your plans for the wedding?" Alice looked puzzled. "You know, a large or small one, church or elopement. What about brides-maids and all that?"

"I don't know. I've been too high to think about details." Alice made an exaggerated groan. "My poor client. He didn't get my full attention today. That's for sure. I've been useless. All I think about is Ted and our getting married."

They fell into earnest conversation as Alice related the details of the proposal. They didn't stop until the waiter placed cool salads in front of them. After a few bites, Alice inquired, "What about you? I can't believe you're taking this suspension nonsense so calmly."

"Worrying about it won't help." Erika sipped her wine. "I took Macomber a letter yesterday morning explaining my actions and begging his forgiveness."

"You didn't?"

Erika shrugged. "The DA suggested I do it. He hopes the letter will placate Macomber and squelch a DBA review."

A quick flash of annoyance passed over Alice's face. "In your case, the suspension is more than enough. What do they want, blood?"

Erika finished all the salad she wanted and placed her fork on the plate. "It appears so."

"And what do you intend to do about it?"

"All I can do. Wait. I retained Mitch, and he helped with the letter. Macomber told me he would let me know what he expects to do tomorrow. If he chooses to press the charge, Mitch will represent me with the board."

Alice drank some wine and ate some salad. "Can I help you?"

Erika shook her head. "No. Waiting is my job and I deserve it, but if things get hot, I'll want you to hold my hand."

Alice looked long and hard at her. "You're taking this too well. What's happened?"

Erika smiled. "You always know how I feel, don't you?"

"Not always. I expected you to be hitting the skids by now, but you're not."

"Yesterday and today, I've thought seriously about my future. My dedication to the law caused me to miss so much and I've been considering a change." Alice choked slightly on a bite of salad. "After seeing the family attorney, I have enough money to last for a year, maybe two, if I'm frugal. I might take time and see some of the world, or open my own law office. I don't know yet. Maybe it's time to quit being a slave and learn how to enjoy life. Who knows?"

"Hear, hear," Alice exclaimed. "I'll drink to any or all of that." She raised her glass for another toast.

Erika was truly happy for her friend, and more grateful than ever for her friendship. "It was nice of you not to raise a fuss over what I just told you. For some reason I thought you might think I was a quitter and be upset."

"Erika, my dear, nothing could upset me today." Alice smiled warmly. "If it makes you happy, I'm happy."

They decided their agreement called for another toast. Alice summoned the waiter and he poured a second glass of wine.

They ate quietly, savoring each bite. Erika remembered their phone conversation. "You told me the exciting news. Now bring me up to date on the office gossip."

Alice shrugged and made a small face. "Just rumors about the hearing. You know your office and mine. There's always someone or something to talk about."

"What about the hearing?"

"Fireworks is the word." Alice gulped more wine. "I don't think it's going in Josh's favor right now."

"That's not news. I could've told you that. Mitch called yesterday. He sounded down. He phoned, then barely said a half-dozen words. He told me his mind was on the hearing."

Alice was blunt. "Erika, do you know what a throwaway is?"

Suspecting a joke, she said. "Something you throw away, I guess. What's the catch?"

"No joke. It's a term the police use. It refers to an extra gun some policemen carry. The fireworks is kind of a pun they're using at the office. It refers to a gun. Rumor has it Josh carried a throwaway."

"Back up, Alice, and explain. You're too far ahead of me."

Alice wiggled and drank more wine. She spread the fingers of her hands on each side of her plate emphasizing her story. To Erika, she sounded like a bad actor. "Street policemen sometimes carry an extra gun. If they have trouble with someone, they can plant the gun on the victim to protect themselves. They claim the victim had a gun and excessive force was necessary." Erika noticed that as Alice spoke the ham performance faded. "It's not ethical, but some policemen carry throwaways with the rationalization that they need a hidden gun just in case a suspect disarms them. The rumor at the office is, Josh carries a throwaway."

The significance of Alice's story was apparent to Erika. "You're telling me Kimball was right. Rick didn't have a gun. It was Josh's extra weapon."

"I said no such thing. All I know is, they're whispering in my office Josh carries an extra gun. No one ventured to speculate about his use of it. The certainty is, if Josh carries the gun, it makes him look bad. And if he looks bad, it makes Mitch's job much harder."

"Maybe it should," Erika said, with ire.

Alice struck the table lightly. "Erika, if you let this spoil our evening I'll never tell you anything again."

Erika smiled. "Not a chance. We're here to celebrate and that, my dear, is exactly what we're going to do." They drank another toast and talked for a long time, making wedding plans.

Erika drove the car conscientiously going home, too much wine, shared happiness and celebration had gone to her head. As she parked her car, she spotted Mitch's Bronco in a guest spot and saw him in the park, sitting on a bench near one of the lights. Except for him, the park was deserted. He didn't hear her as she approached, nor was he startled when she spoke. "Hello there, counselor."

He held out his hand and pulled her down next to him. "I've been waiting for you," he said, as he placed his arm around her shoulders and held her firmly. "Dare I ask where you were?"

"Celebrating," she answered smugly.

"Celebrating?"

"With Alice. Ted proposed to her last night. They're going to be married." She turned to watch his face.

His eyes twinkled and he sounded genuinely enthusiastic. "Good for them. Parsons is a lucky man. Alice is a striking

126

woman, and she's your friend, so I hope they'll be very happy."

Erika snuggled closer. "So do I." She giggled remembering her evening. "I've never seen Alice happier and it's contagious. We ate and drank and gossiped just like we used to do. And the plans we made—you wouldn't believe all the planning we did. It was a happy time for a change, and I feel good."

He laughed quietly and she felt the pressure of his arm tighten. "I can tell you're happy, and it's time something good happened to you." He bent and kissed her. Erika felt the stirring inside her. Her response was involuntary and she relaxed, melting to him. She heard his heavy breathing before he withdrew and held her face in his hands. "Can you think of a way we might continue the celebration?"

She lowered her eyes and sighed. "Yes, I can." She twisted away from his hands. "You know you drive me crazy."

"You know you affect me the same way," he said huskily. Releasing her and turning away, he spoke. "You expect too much, Erika."

"What do I expect?" she whispered.

He hung his head and looked down. "You want me to delay making love to you. It's destined to happen. Why tease me? You expect me to say I love you before we make love."

"I don't think that's expecting too much."

"All women want you to tell them you love them before you take them to bed. It makes them feel better about what they want to do anyway."

"I'm not all women," she said flatly. "Since it's 'hate Erika' night, is there anything else?" The difficulty she had asking the question came from the hurt grabbing at her insides. There was a certain cynicism in her voice. "Well?"

"I'm no superman Erika, I make mistakes too." He leaned back, looking at the sky. "Why did all this have to happen now?" he groaned.

Erika gazed at him for a long moment without answering. Neither of them moved. She could hear the wind blowing in the trees. "I'm not a child, Mitch," she said. "I'm responsible for my actions. I wish I weren't suspended, but it happened. I want to learn about Rick. I hope I do. Yet, I don't intend to let it destroy me. I'm a big girl now. I can take it."

"I know," he mumbled. He turned to look at her. "Yesterday and today, I've been in a panic, thinking you might leave me. You told me once if . . ."

"Oh Mitch," she said impatiently. "Don't you understand? I love you. I'm telling you. I love you."

He studied her for a long tense moment. "You picked a hell of a time to tell me. Erika, the hearing has gone bad, and I'm afraid of losing. . . ."

She stopped his words when her fingers found his lips. "How long ago was it I said, 'Yes, I can think of a way to continue tonight's celebration?' I don't want to hear about the hearing or anything but us." She looked into his astonished face. "How does that grab you, counselor?"

He gathered her into his arms and his kiss was fierce. When he finished, he whispered. "Shall we go?"

The phone was ringing as Erika unlocked her apartment door. She hurried to answer it, a habit born of all those months of hoping a late-night call might be from Rick. Mitch's "Don't answer it!" came too late. He watched her, as with head bowed she listened to her caller. After a moment, she said "yes" in a flat voice and hung up.

"Well, what is it?"

"You're right, I shouldn't have answered. It was Dick Renquist. He's been trying to reach me all evening." She sighed. There was probably another explosion coming—might as well walk right in. "He's ten minutes away and he's coming over. He didn't tell me why, but he's on his way." She eyed Mitch warily.

"Do you want me to go and come back later?" He didn't explode after all.

"No, stay. I need you."

He beamed at her. "Yes ma'am. I think I'll make me a drink. May I fix one for you?" She shook her head and sat down to wait while he went to the kitchen.

Mitch returned, sitting down near her, armed with a large drink. "Did Renquist give you any clues?"

"No, but he sounded upset. He may be coming here to fire me."

Mitch turned away. "You didn't do anything stupid today, did you?"

Erika made an aggravated face. "Nothing new," she answered.

He chuckled. "Then he's not coming here at this time of night to fire you. Office hours are reserved for dismissals."

She felt the corner of her mouth twitch. "Dick won't fire me. He might pressure me to resign, but he won't fire me." She shifted around and leaned on him. "Not too many days ago, the thought of resigning or being fired threw me into a panic. Now, it hardly matters. It just isn't important."

Mitch set his glass on the table and gathered her to him. "What changed your mind?" he asked as they adjusted their bodies to accommodate each other.

"I've been doing a lot of thinking. My life hasn't been what it should. I'm appalled to think of the hours I've spent working so hard just for a chance to work even harder. There has to be more to life than that." She rested her head on his chest. "I came into some money today. It's helped relieve the pressure."

He stroked her hair softly and ignored her statement about the money. She should have known money wouldn't matter to him. "What do you want from life, then?" he asked.

"Happiness," she told him honestly.

"It's only been recently you've been unhappy. Don't chuck everything you've worked for. Events are bound to improve. You're proud of your work, and you're a damned good lawyer."

She cuddled to his shoulder, resting her head. "I'm positive if I stay in law, I must make some changes, either in my attitude, or a change of employment."

"Can you change your attitude? That's the most important modification, and the most difficult one."

"Why do you think you're here, counselor?"

Mitch's face beamed. No small, crooked grin, but a huge smile, filled his face before he told her, "I know why I'm here." He looked into her eyes intently, searching for something. Finding it, he kissed her. He sat back and cleared his throat. "Give your profession another chance, Erika. I believe you'd be lost without it. Listen to me," he said impatiently. "I can't believe I'm trying to sell you on the law. Remember, the law was responsible for our meeting."

She smiled. "Meeting you was the high point of all those years. Perhaps if I'd joined the public defender's office instead of the DA's, I'd feel differently."

"That's doubtful," he said nuzzling his face in her hair. "You'd be crazy to take that job."

"Why?"

"You know how people are. They believe you get what you pay for. Since they can't pay and their lawyer is assigned to them, they think they don't have a capable attorney. They hate you for it."

"I suppose you're right. You didn't have my problem did you? You always had your own practice."

"Yup. Having money can be an advantage, and I frankly admit I enjoy it. Like you, if I had to make a choice, I would've chosen the office you did."

"You have defended some guilty people, haven't you?"

His breathing was sharp and irregular. His answer was a gasp. "Certainly," he whispered as he began to trail tiny kisses along her neck.

She tried to seem unaffected, but her throaty murmur gave her away. "Did you know they were guilty?"

"Of course," he groaned. "Hell, Erika, don't talk now." His mouth found hers, and her body caught fire.

Struggling to breathe, she wrenched her mouth from his. "I'm sorry I answered the phone." He didn't respond with words.

The doorbell rang. Mitch straightened up, took a deep breath and pushed back his tousled hair. He smiled slightly, walked to the kitchen, found his suit coat, and went to the door. Erika straightened her dress and tossed her head, forcing her hair to fall into place. Mitch paused, turned and smiled. "Ready?"

"Ready," she answered.

# Chapter Ten

MITCH OPENED THE door and stepped aside, saying, "Come in, Dick." Renquist paused and looked flustered. A hint of red appeared on his face. He glanced nervously around the room, looked at Erika, then turned to Mitch and offered his hand. "I apologize if I'm interrupting, but I need to talk with Erika." Their handshake was short but friendly, and Dick managed a faint smile.

Erika smiled, enjoying Dick's confusion. "Come sit down," she said. "You aren't disturbing us."

He chose the chair across from her. "I know it's late to come calling, but I had to speak to you before you read the story in tomorrow's papers." He glanced at Mitch. "I tried to call you earlier." He sighed and rubbed his creased forehead. "It's not good news for any of us."

Her first thought, as soon as she had seen his face, was of her job. Erika reached for Mitch's hand. "You've heard from Macomber, haven't you?" she said. His remark about the paper registered after she spoke. Surely her suspension and possible probation wouldn't have made the news.

"Yes, but . . . yes I did."

"Well?"

"He's going the whole distance. You'll have to answer before a bar review board."

Mitch covered her hand with his. "We hoped this wouldn't happen, but we're not worried about it." She looked at him and agreed silently. Renquist cleared his throat and continued to look worried.

"Would my resignation stop the proceedings?" Erika questioned.

"Probably not. Macomber wants this on your record. Even if you quit our office, you're still a lawyer and you'd be working somewhere." Renquist looked devastated. "Erika . . ."

She broke in. "Do you want me to resign?"

Mitch sucked in his breath sharply. "Don't offer to resign. You handed him the advantage, Erika. Think how easy it is for him to say yes. Never make it easy for an employer to fire you."

Erika looked surprised. "What difference does it make? If it makes it easier for Dick, I'll do it." Mitch frowned and opened his mouth to say something, but didn't. She appreciated his advice, but she owed Renquist, even if she paid the debt with her job.

"Erika." Her eyes went first to Dick and then to Mitch. Each had said her name at the same time. Mitch nodded to Renquist.

"I don't want you to resign. I never did." He stopped, hung his head. "Damn it, I'm not here because of Macomber. I'm here about Josh Manning." Mitch dropped her hand and glared at him. Dick met his gaze. "Don't worry, Mitch. I'm not doing anything unethical."

"I hope not," Mitch snapped. "But right now it doesn't look that way." His face changed to its closed and stern lawyer expression. "Accept my apology, Dick. My remark was out of line."

Erika was curious, and she couldn't hide her impatience. "What is it, Dick?"

"New evidence. We issued a warrant for Manning's arrest earlier this evening."

Erika sucked in her breath sharply, astonished by his statement. Mitch stood, glowering. "You have Manning in jail?"

Renquist shook his head. "No. He ran. He's disappeared, and we can't find him. No one has seen him since the hearing earlier today."

Erika closed her eyes. The wine she'd had at dinner dulled

her mind, or she'd missed something. She reached for Mitch's hand, and tugged at him until he sat beside her. "Both of you know more about this than I. Isn't it about time you enlightened me?"

Dick's eyes questioned Mitch, who thought for several moments as the tension mounted. Finally he asked, "Are you certain Manning has disappeared?" Dick nodded. Mitch went to the phone, called his answering service, then his house in Vail. He turned to Renquist. "When did you discover he was gone?"

"Around six this evening."

Mitch consulted his watch. "It's been well over five hours then, and he hasn't tried to contact me." He turned to Erika and half smiled. "Apparently I don't have a client after all. You warned me. I should've listened to you. You get your wish, and I'm glad to be out of it." His crooked smile appeared. "Next time, I'll listen to your intuition." Before she could tell him it didn't matter, he turned away. "I'll get us a drink before we start this recital. I think all of us could use a nerve-steadier." He disappeared into the kitchen, then returned promptly, passed around the drinks and settled down with a sigh. "Who starts, Dick? You or I?" Dick deferred with a dour look and a slight salute with his glass.

Erika could no longer stand the suspense. "Both of you are so aggravating, sitting there complacent and all-knowing. Please, one of you, tell me about Josh."

Dick sipped his drink. Mitch smiled at him. "Feel free to correct me or jump in any time you wish." Erika considered screaming to get them to get on with it. Mitch began. "Well, Erika, it seems your boss and the city police department did an outstanding piece of investigative work. Our friend Manning is a crook, and possibly a murderer."

Erika felt no shock or anger, only dismay. "He killed Rick intentionally?"

"More than likely. A confession would be necessary to convict him of murder, and he has no intention of confessing, although running as he has is almost as good. It appears to be an admission of guilt.''

Erika shifted uncomfortably. "I can't believe Josh meant to kill Rick. He didn't know my brother. You don't kill people you don't know . . . unless you're a psycho.''

Dick placed his drink on the table and leaned towards them. "We believe Josh knew your brother before he knew you.''

"You said *believe*. You don't *know*, do you?''

"Stop trying to defend him,'' Mitch said, his words tinged with disdain. "Dick's guess is more than an educated one, and he's probably right.''

Like a computer, her mind searched her memory banks, stopping when they reached Ty Kimball. "Kimball told you about Janey?''

Dick nodded. "She's a very stubborn young lady. We spent many hours with her.'' He smiled. "Miss Langley told us what she told you. I'm sorry, Erika, we haven't convinced her you didn't rat on her.''

"I'm surprised you believed her.''

"At first I didn't, but we started looking into what she said. For two days our investigators combed the schools.'' He retrieved his drink and Mitch pulled her closer to him, squeezing her shoulder. "Manning is running the same scam now. At least he did up until the shooting. We have three witnesses who will testify to it and implicate him. That was enough to issue the warrant. We'll probably find more evidence and willing witnesses, but we had enough to ask for the warrant today.''

She slumped against Mitch. "Manning is Renegade Rat? He's been involved in theft and burglary for over two years?''

"Honestly, Erika we can't prove he's been at it for years, we just know he's been doing it lately. As for the past, yes, I think he was the man who assisted your brother and his friends.''

"Did you suspect him before the shooting?''

"I wish we could say yes, but no way,'' Renquist answered.

Josh had an impeccable record. I didn't suspect him at all until just before the grand jury investigation.''

His face reddened when Erika snapped, ''Then it did start as a political ploy?'' Renquist's face became redder, and she glanced at Mitch, who revealed a small smile. She nodded to acknowledge it.

Dick dropped his eyes. ''I wouldn't use those words, but something like them. What difference does it make? The grand jury produced results.''

Erika repressed a strange desire to laugh. ''Tell me what changed your mind.'' Busy pouting, Dick didn't wish to go on. He looked at Mitch, silently asking him to take over.

''Manning carried an extra gun. Dick found several policemen who knew about it. Josh obviously wasn't too careful. Wherever he is, he's wishing he had been more discreet about the throwaway. Officer Jackson was with him the night he shot your brother. He identified the gun on the scene as the same kind and caliber as Josh's throwaway.''

''I knew it. I knew the gun was important, just as soon as . . .'' She stopped abruptly.

Mitch's eyebrows lifted. ''You knew about the gun. How?''

''Never mind.'' Her tone was biting, but she squirmed under his gaze. ''Sorry, but I can't tell you.'' Two sets of eyes stared at her. ''Forget it. Bring more charges if you want, but I won't tell you.'' Mitch chuckled and Dick groaned. They both eyed her for a long moment before they gave up and Renquist continued the story.

''After Manning's throwaway was discovered and identified as his, our office decided there might be more to the story. I asked permission to talk to Kimball.'' He gave Erika a stern look. ''And got it. I spent three hours with him. He told me over and over about you, Erika, and the events of the shooting. I was about to give up when he mentioned Janey.''

''You're lucky. He didn't remember her last name for me,'' Erika said wistfully. ''I had to remember it on my own.''

"For me either, but we sent a couple of men to Rick's school asking questions."

Erika shrugged. "All you had to do was come to me. I would've told you."

Renquist smiled. "Did you know Janey isn't a popular name these days, and hasn't been for a number of years? In all those students, for the past three years there was only one. And that's about it, Erika. You know the rest."

She sighed. "Will you get us another drink, Mitch? I need time to let this soak in."

Dick stood. "Not for me, thanks. I must go. Sorry, Erika— we shouldn't have let Manning slip away—and sorry we can't charge him with murder." He hung his head and shifted his weight. "But you can be sure, when we get him, he'll spend a long time in the state pen." He looked down at the floor. "God, the office is going to have trouble when the word gets out Manning is a crook, and we let him get away." He turned to Mitch. "I'll see you in the morning at the hearing. It won't last long. Your client won't be there, and after I present the new evidence, it'll all be over."

Mitch walked him to the door, and shook his hand again. "I never enjoy losing, but you did a fine bit of work, and Erika has waited long enough for a solution about her brother. This time, I'm happy to lose." They exchanged good-nights and Renquist left.

Absorbed in thought, Erika didn't know how much time passed before Mitch nudged her arm and handed her the drink she'd requested. "You're really out of it, aren't you?" he said.

She took the drink and sipped it. "How much of this did you know, Mitch?"

"About the gun and Janey. I don't know much about the crime ring operation, just enough to be suspicious. I can't believe Manning could pull it off; yet, he kept it up for a long time. How rotten can you get, using kids that way?"

"It's difficult to believe he could get away with it all this time."

"He probably cooled it at times and moved around from school to school. I guess he had to be smart, or he would've been caught months ago."

"I wish he had been." Erika smiled, then pressed her lips together hard. She sat that way for a while. "It really is ironic. Josh is running now, just like Rick did."

Mitch stroked her arm. "But it's *over*. It's all finished business now."

"Not really. There's tomorrow's papers. I wonder just how much of the story they know."

"We'll see tomorrow."

Again, Erika fell into deep thought. Her lips smiled sadly. "Strange isn't it? Josh wasn't my friend. He kept in touch with me and bought me dinners and took me along with him when he looked for Rick because he had to know if Rick came home or got in touch with me. He knew I'd tell him." She finished her drink in one gulp. "Before I met you, I thought I only had two close friends, Josh and Alice." A half-laugh, half-sob passed her lips.

"You aren't going to cry, are you? He isn't worth it. You knew him longer than I, but he snowed us both. Manning could sell feathers to chickens." His voice had a hint of admiration in it. "He was slick."

Erika didn't cry, she laughed quietly. "Do you think the police will catch him?"

Mitch considered the question. "He's smart, but police all over the country will be looking for him. They don't like cops who go bad and give them a bum name. They'll be looking for him around every corner." He paused and kissed her cheek. "Life isn't going to be easy for Manning." From the look on his face, Mitch was mulling something over before he spoke. "I'm puzzled. Did Manning know Rick was back in town? Did he know exactly what he was doing when he fired at your brother, or did he shoot an unarmed kid to discover it was Rick later?"

Erika didn't answer immediately. Everything was clear to her. "Can't accept the coincidence?" she asked.

His face softened. "I can accept it. I believe the wilder the story, the more likely it's true." He became thoughtful. "A jury might recognize the difference between the two events."

"Trust a defense attorney to look for an out. Of course Josh recognized Rick. Did Jackson hear two shots?" Mitch nodded slowly. "Josh fired the throwaway, shot Rick with his service revolver, placed the extra gun in his hand . . ." She paused and questioned Mitch. "Rick's fingerprints were on the throwaway?"

"They were," he answered.

"Everything Josh did could be accomplished in a matter of seconds. I don't believe you'd have a prayer of convincing a jury Josh didn't know it was Rick."

His hand ran through her hair, mussing it. He smiled broadly. "And I think you're right."

"You weren't puzzled at all." Erika accused and his eyes twinkled. "You just wanted to be certain I understood."

Mitch nodded. "Absolutely. You should know how it happened. Accepting it won't be any easier, but you should know. Settle it in your mind and don't waste your time stewing about it again."

"We were both wrong about so many things. Does that shake your confidence some?"

"Maybe, but I can't afford to worry about it. I'm right much more often than I'm wrong. That's what counts."

She cuddled into his shoulder and changed the subject. "I'm sorry about Janey. I would like to help her, if she'd let me." He held her close and didn't answer, but she heard him sigh. "She loved Rick enough she considered running away with him." Erika adjusted her body to his and snuggled tighter. "Did Janey talk about Rick at the hearing?"

He shook his head. "She's a wary one. When questions were asked, she would answer as briefly as she could."

"I imagine it was difficult for her to testify about the robbery ring."

Mitch adjusted his weight. "There weren't too many questions concerning it. I certainly didn't ask any, since it was a complete surprise to me, and Dick only pursued it enough to impress the panel."

"Then you don't know how Rick got involved?"

"No," he answered, as his arms tightened around her.

"Janey said it was a dumb school initiation. In order to be in a club, you had to steal something. I gathered it turned into some stupid match between two clubs and they competed over the amount of money they made."

He took a long breath. "Sounds impossible, doesn't it? I know kids do bizarre things at times, but this almost tops anything I've heard." He let his breath out slowly. "I do know of several small businesses, most of them near schools, that went under because of all the shoplifting. The kids wiped them out."

"How do you feel about my brother?"

"Oh, Erika, I don't know. Angry, I guess, because he put you through all this. I didn't know him and I don't intend to pass judgment. Once was enough."

"What's going to happen to Kimball?" she wondered out loud.

"He's a sad case, isn't he?"

"I feel so sorry for him. He needs help, Mitch."

"Don't suggest I help him. I've enjoyed about as much as I can stand of this whole matter."

Her eyes pleaded. "Please?"

"Oh no, you don't. I refuse to be dragged into it. No way, not even for you."

"He's so frightened. You could . . ."

"I can find someone to help him. That's all I'll do."

"Thanks, counselor," she whispered and smiled, her eyes proposing a delicious invitation.

Mitch moved and stretched out, pulling her down with him. His mouth sought her ear and he whispered, "Your brother was lucky to have a beautiful, intelligent sister like you."

"I'm not a living, breathing success story at the moment. Remember Macomber?"

"He's a minor inconvenience." Mitch lifted her head and looked into her eyes. "I was lucky to get out of this and still have you. You mean more to me than any job. Nothing is worth losing you."

Happiness filled her. Her voice was low and throaty. "This minute, I don't want to remember anything but you." He kissed her earlobe and started down her neck, sparking fire with every touch. "*Ooooooh*," she murmured, "you do that well." She heard him *hummmmmm* as he kissed her with uninhibited desire. He pulled her up and guided her down the hall, pausing only to take the phone off the hook.

In the dim light of early morning, Erika woke and gazed at the man sleeping quietly and soundly beside her. Reaching out, she traced his ear lightly with her finger, then touched his lips. Behind the memory of his caresses came the unwelcome awareness that even during the heat of their passion he hadn't told her he loved her. Yet, she knew he did. Well, she was almost certain. Her hand trailed aimlessly down his neck to his chest. Spreading her fingers, she felt his hard muscles, his body rising and falling ever so slightly as he breathed, and the solid thump of his heart. She was going to love this man, if he never said he loved her. Cuddling to him, she rested her head and finally fell asleep.

Two hours later, she roused when she heard his voice. "Erika!" He gently touched her cheek. "Erika, wake up. It's late. We overslept and I have to be at that damned hearing in an hour."

Slowly, she rolled over to look at him. "Good morning, counselor," she murmured in a teasing way.

"Good morning. Did you hear me? Get up. I'm late."

Erika yawned and stretched. "Your logic escapes me. Why should I get up? I'm not late." She held out her hand and held it there until he took it. "Kiss me," she said softly.

Willing to oblige, he slipped back beside her and his kiss was filled with love and tenderness. "I can think of more entertaining business than the hearing," she invited.

He moaned and drew back to look at her. His brown eyes glistened. "So can I." His next kiss was not so tender, and she nestled against him. Without a word, he leaped from the bed and started for the shower. "Come back here, Mitchell Logan. You can't leave me like this," she demanded.

"Have to go," he drawled and proceeded to strut the rest of the way to the shower, whistling as he went.

Ten minutes later the water in the shower still ran. Erika found her best peignoir, gave her hair a quick brush, and ran to the kitchen to start the coffee. In no time, he stood near her ready to leave. He smiled wryly. "Do you suppose Renquist will recognize the suit? I wore it last night and I don't have time to go by my office and change."

She handed him some coffee and laughed cheerfully. "I can see Dick now, calling your clothes to everyone's attention. He'll walk up to you and say loudly, 'I see you spent the night at Erika's. You forgot to change, old chap.' "

He screwed up his face and gulped the coffee. "Stay here this morning and get a bag packed. I'll call you as soon as I can." He kissed her goodbye, smiling a satisfied smile.

Erika was pleased it was Friday. Another weekend lay before them. She packed a bag with jeans, shirts and sweaters, showered and dressed carefully, brushing her hair until it shone.

Mitch called at ten. "How did the hearing go?" she queried rather hesitantly.

"Just about the way Renquist said it would. The panel was excused about fifteen minutes ago and it's all over. By the way, before I forget—the police traced Manning to the airport. He boarded a plane for Detroit before anyone knew he was gone. I bet he headed for Canada."

"I read the story in the papers. They didn't say he left town, but that's the only bit of information they missed. The *Post* had the entire story.'' She made an effort to keep any hint of melancholy out of her voice, but didn't succeed.

"Don't feel badly, Erika. We're getting out of town where we can leave it behind. I expect to leave the office around one. Be ready.''

"I'm packed. All I need is you.''

"One more thing. Did Macomber call?''

"No. He said he would, but I haven't heard from him. It doesn't matter, does it? Dick told us last night what to expect.''

He sounded impatient. "True, but if the man's going to keep his word, he should call.''

"Mitch. It's not noon yet. Macomber thinks he has the whole day, and he does. Stop bothering about it. I'm not worried. Stop chatting and finish your work so we can be on our way.''

He laughed heartily. "I'm working, I'm working. Remember, be ready shortly after one.''

Erika occupied her time cleaning an apartment which didn't need cleaning. Three times she tried to get in touch with Alice, but failed. On the final try, she left a message saying she would be in Vail for the weekend.

Just about on time, Mitch arrived, kissed her and pushed her out the door. "Hurry,'' he said. "A cab is waiting outside.''

He walked close behind her, herding her through the hall. "Why a cab? What's wrong with the Bronco?''

"Nothing, I just don't want to leave it at the airport.'' She almost trotted in front of him as he continued to hurry her. "I'll tell you all about it after we get in the cab.''

She settled in the back seat of the taxi and they were on their way. She turned to him. "Well?''

"We're not going to Vail. We're going to Las Vegas for the weekend. A little warm weather and sunshine will be nice, and best of all, we'll get away from Denver and the problems.'' He settled next to her and his arm circled her shoulders. "A special trip will be nice.''

Again, old habits were hard to break and she began to object automatically. "I can't go to Vegas. I didn't pack the right clothes; I told Alice I was going to Vail; the weather is absolutely beautiful here, and . . ." She stopped, looking at his amused expression. She smiled. "And I can go, can't I?" He nodded slightly before he kissed her. She nestled to him, considering her actions. She'd spent the night with him, so it hardly mattered if they went to Vegas together. Raising her head, she looked at his marvelous face, then kissed him. "I hope you like jeans at posh casinos. I only packed casual attire." He kissed her again, laughing at the same time.

# Chapter Eleven

THE TAXI STOPPED away from the main terminal of Stapleton Airport. Erika stepped out and admired the cool, clear, beautiful day. She breathed deeply and her face wrinkled when she smelled the kerosene lingering in the air. Mitch waited until the cabbie handed him the bags from the trunk, then paid him. She made a mental note to ask him later about his bag, it was big, much larger than hers.

Erika took his arm. "I hate to appear stupid," she remarked, "but we won't find a plane out here. Why did we get out of the cab?"

Sounding a trifle aggravated, he turned her around. "We'll find one over there. We're taking my plane."

She looked back at him, "Sorry . . ."

"You didn't forget I have my own plane, did you?" Before she could answer, he said, "You must do something about your memory." His dark hair moved in the breeze and his deep gaze was difficult to meet. Curling his lips, he whispered, "We both did some flying last night." He lowered his mouth to hers. Stepping back, he lifted the bags and they walked across the street to a one-story building with a private hangar; a red and white plane rested in front.

"That's your plane?"

He grinned and nodded. "Yup. I bought it in a moment of madness."

Kidding him to hide her ignorance and the fear that this plane wasn't sturdy enough to fulfill its task, she said, "I thought your plane would be a jet."

His laughter filled the air before he spoke. "I love being

overestimated. It feeds my ego, but Erika, I must admit, I'm not that important." He paused and chuckled quietly. "I can see I have some teaching to do. For starters, jets cost several million dollars, and flying them requires a rating I couldn't maintain. I simply don't have the time."

Erika faked a pout. "How disappointing."

"This plane makes more sense. I can fly to small airports in little towns when I have business there."

She continued to needle him. "First, I expected an Alfa Romeo and got a Bronco. I want a Lear jet and I get a . . . a . . ." She stopped to giggle. "What am I getting?"

"A Cessna One Eighty-two, commonly called a Skylane. It's a high-performance, retractable gear . . ."

She almost choked on her laughter and pointed to the plane. "That's a lot of name for such a little airplane." Erika leaned against him, resting her head on his shoulder. "Well, I can say Bronco and Cessna. I'll trust you to know the rest."

"You could learn it too, Erika." Her head jerked to see him congratulate himself. "What a great idea! You should learn to fly!"

His comment was matter of fact. As if he took being able to fly for granted. "Me, fly!" she said in disbelief, and swallowed the lump in her throat.

"Why not? It's great. You'll love it. Flying saves time, it's exciting, exhilarating and all sorts of good things. Provided you learn, we could fly this machine anywhere in the country. Think about it, just the two of us traveling anywhere we wanted to go." His face glowed just talking about it. They approached the plane, and he nodded his head approvingly. "Isn't she beautiful?"

Erika's mouth dropped open. She couldn't speak. He dreamed big dreams. Eventually she smiled, agreeing the plane was beautiful.

Aboard his expensive toy, Erika was still preoccupied with its size. But even if it wasn't very large, it looked awfully complex and expensive. She had only been on an airplane three times in her life, always a commercial jumbo jet. This cabin was spacious, with room for two more in a back seat, and a baggage compartment behind that, but compared to a 747, it was *tiny*. Mitch stowed their luggage, then walked all the way around the plane, checking this and that. He seemed to know what he was doing. After a few minutes, he opened her door and touched her shoulder. "I need to see a man in the office. I'll be right back and we'll be on our way."

Erika settled back in her seat and took a deep breath. The plane was another symbol of the differences between them. She looked out the window, her fingers curled into fists, and her heart began to hammer. She was aware of how desperately she wanted to please him and compressed her lips. The moment of truth had come, her life was about to change dramatically. As she glanced at her reflection in the window, she smiled with satisfaction. Rick's money enabled her to feel less intimidated by Mitch, and after last night, he couldn't bully or browbeat her again. She could identify with letting loose and kicking up her heels. She was going to enjoy her new lifestyle. Resting her head on the bulkhead, she waited happily for him to return.

Mitch climbed through the door, tossed his coat and tie aside and settled into the pilot's seat. "Ready?"

"Vegas, here we come," she said, sounding as happy as she looked. Mitch leaned over her and kissed her hair. "We're going to have a marvelous time."

Her tongue moistened her lips. "I'm sure we will," she said, experiencing an unsteady mixture of anticipation and nervousness. He began checking the instrument panel. Erika didn't know if she should disturb this process, but after a few moments, she risked it. "How long have you been planning this trip?"

"Since last night," he answered without looking her way.

Her eyes lingered on him. "You managed a lot in a short time."

He reached out and thumped a finger on one of the dials. "Oh, I didn't do it. Mrs. O'Brien or someone at my office made the arrangements."

She wondered why he always took people for granted, expecting them to please him. "This isn't the dark ages. It surprises me your office personnel doesn't resent doing your private business for you."

His remark seemed cold. "I pay them well. If they don't like it, they can find employment elsewhere."

"Mitch! You don't mean that?"

"Of course I do." He seemed to think for a moment. "With one disclaimer. I would hate losing Mrs. O'Brien. She's a gem and one humdinger when it comes to managing the office. I suppose if she complained about doing personal things for me, I wouldn't ask her to do them." He paused. "Maybe I should hire a personal secretary."

Erika huffed inside. In a perverse way, she was caught in one giant philosophical disagreement. When she thought they were equal, they were opposite. Gritting her teeth, she remained silent and drifted inside herself. He went where he wanted, bought what he wanted, even obedient employees. Easing back in the seat, she felt better telling herself he couldn't buy her. Remembering several conflicts when she had deferred to his wishes left her aggravated. Why did she give in to him so easily? Then, there was last night. Beautiful last night. They were together in every way. "Huh?" she mumbled when he spoke to her.

"Are you ready? It's time to go."

They taxied for what seemed a short time. The plane bounced along the ground in a manner she thought eager. Soon enough, they waited before the concrete runway. Mitch listened to his head-set, nodded and said something she didn't hear above the sound of the engines. Uncertain for her safety in this small machine, she watched Mitch, then looked outside to see everything around them passing too fast. Engrossed in the take-off, Mitch said nothing. His eyes sparkled and his face was expressionless. Suddenly, they were airborne in a steep climb; one turn and they raced towards the mountains.

"How long will this take?" she questioned, proud her voice was steady.

"A few hours from now we'll be safe in our hotel room in Las Vegas thinking about making love."

"Mitch!"

"Why not? I'm already thinking about it. As a matter of fact, I thought about it all morning. In a few minutes when we're on auto pilot, I might even consider giving it a try."

Wide-eyed, she raised her voice to a higher pitch. "You wouldn't?"

"No, but I'll think about it. You're incredible in the bedroom, but I'd be surprised if you didn't know that. Your willingness to please is fantastic." His eyes burned like small candles. "Most women want to be pleased, they don't care about pleasing."

Anger and jealousy flared. "You'd know more about that than I," she rasped.

"Yes, ma'am!"

His answer irked her more and she looked down. She couldn't get the message she wanted together. Mitch pointed down. "That's Dillon Lake coming up."

"So soon?"

"I fly a fast, mean machine, lady." Soon he adjusted their course. She had watched long enough, and knowing the location of the lake, knew they turned south. Silently she watched. A few more minutes and he negotiated another turn to the west. He switched on the auto pilot and looked into her eyes, searching them. She hoped he wouldn't see the last dregs of anger there. "It didn't take you long to adjust, Erika. I'm proud of you."

"How did you know I was concerned?"

He chuckled. "Elementary, my dear. You looked plain

scared. When did you make the decision to trust me?''

"When I considered the consequences if I became hysterical up here alone with you.''

His arm found her shoulder and caressed it. "That's my girl.'' They gazed at each other for what seemed an age. She grew warm and squirmed, remembering his threat of a few minutes ago. Somehow he read her mind, and sighed. She decided to change the subject. "You don't seem the Vegas type. Why did you choose it?''

"Ordinarily I don't care much for the place, yet it has charm. Even if you don't gamble, there's so many things to do. You need to be in the mood for it, and I guess I am.'' He did something to one of the knobs on the control panel. "Do you gamble?''

"Rarely,'' she admitted. "Oh, I remember. I wanted to ask about your bag. You're carrying enough for a week. What's in there?''

"Clothes, mostly. I brought my tux to match your jeans,'' he teased.

Her voice was surly. "We'll make a lovely couple.''

"I don't doubt it, but you never know when an occasion may arise calling for formal attire.''

"If it does, you'll go alone. I don't have anything to wear.''

"Can't do that,'' he drawled. "We have an invitation to a bash at the home of a friend of mine.''

Erika said casually. "I hope Levis and T-shirts are in style.''

"No, it's formal.''

She shook her head and dismay flooded her face. "I spent the morning looking for something to do. I could've been prepared. It would've been better for both of us if you'd told me then.''

"Perhaps, but if you'd gone shopping and held us up, we may not have made it. Look down. Those clouds you see are bringing a storm to Denver.''

She peered down cautiously. "They don't look too ominous.''

"Trust me," he said. "We'll buy you something. Las Vegas has at least a dozen shops that will be happy to outfit you."

Trapped once more, she sighed. "You're forgiven. Who's your friend?"

"Ken Grayson. He and his wife are celebrating their twentieth wedding anniversary."

"That's lovely. Did you buy a gift?"

He screwed up his mouth. "Not yet."

She tossed her head. "Then, we do have some shopping to do." She looked down at the clouds beneath them and he leaned back, looking completely satisfied. They didn't talk again for a few minutes, then he dropped a bomb.

"What would you say if I offered you a partnership in my law firm?"

His unexpected query startled her. She had no answer for him. "You don't have any partners," she said, as her mind raced.

"I know, but there's always a first time. What about it?"

"Are you offering, or speculating?"

"Offering."

"A junior partnership or a full one?"

"Full, and you're in luck, you don't have to buy in. I'm having an extraordinary sale. It's free."

"Nothing is free. You'd expect some kind of payment. Typing or filing maybe? Or dusting and emptying waste baskets?"

"You can do all of those things if you want. I won't stop you. Scrub a few floors if you choose. Who am I to frustrate your domestic instincts?"

"Provided I accept, what kind of cases would you permit me to handle?"

He thought a long moment before his lips curled upwards. "Any and all civil cases involving janitorial services."

"How generous of you," she retorted.

"I thought it was. Glad you agree."

"Come on, Mitch. I can see it now. If your best friend's body was found in the trunk of his wife's car with several bullet holes in him which came from his wife's gun, who would get the case? You or me?''

He pretended to mull over her hypothetical problem. ''That's a hard one to decide.'' His eyebrows came close together. ''You'd get the case. He wouldn't be a friend of mine. Any man who sleeps in the trunk of a car deserves to be shot.''

''You're hopeless,'' she sputtered.

''Don't call your boss hopeless. It's hardly endearing.''

''What do you mean, boss? You said an equal partnership.''

''I don't remember saying equal. I said full partnership.''

''You'd have to change the name of the firm to Wheatly and Logan.''

''Despite your crude attempt to blackmail me, I'll agree to Logan and Wheatly. It's alphabetically sound.''

''You dangle a powerful carrot, counselor.''

''First you nibble on a carrot until you savor its flavor, then you chomp it up.'' Mitch looked at her expectantly.

''The bait is tempting.''

''You'd make me happy if you'd take it.''

Erika wiggled, uncomfortable with her pounding heart. Her weak voice returned. ''Would it work?''

Mitch shrugged. ''Who knows? We could give it a try. Think of all the good things that could happen as a result of the merger.''

''Good for me, you mean. I can't see any advantage for you. I'm a novice compared to you. I can't even contribute much experience.''

''Let me worry about that.''

Erika jumped in. ''I don't want you to worry at all. I'd want to do my share. You shouldn't have to take care of me. I'd want to earn my way.'' After a moment's hesitation, she said, ''I'm capable . . .''

He interrupted curtly. ''You're capable. That's exactly why I want you for a partner.''

She slumped as the air escaped her. Starting to stammer, she began again. ''I don't know. Here I am flying to Vegas, high above the Rocky Mountains with no time to think, and you're proposing something very important to both of us. You confuse me, with your off-the-cuff offer."

His voice rose slightly. "You're intelligent, educated, talented, and beautiful. There's nothing in my practice you can't learn. Have more confidence, Erika. Know you can do it."

She sat silently contemplating his offer, wanting to accept. Her prudent and independent nature forced her to explore the possible results of such a merger. Granted, his offer was an opportunity which would open many doors in her chosen profession. Even if it didn't last, she would gain experience she never dared dream about. It wasn't a step upward; it was a leap. Personally, she couldn't ask for more. Working with the man she loved. What could be better? Deep within, she heard the small irritating voice reciting the negative aspects. Words and phrases intermingled. When the affair is over, is the job? You're gambling. What if your work doesn't please him? Business and pleasure never mix. Be certain, stick with your plan. The voice of her father boomed out clearly: "There's no free lunch. In this world you must work for what you get." Erika knew this wasn't always true. Even her father made mistakes. It was impossible to think rationally. She wanted the partnership. "Mitch, do you really believe I can contribute?"

"Not a doubt in my mind," he answered without hesitation. "I wouldn't have suggested a deal, if I'd had doubts. I need help. I turn down people who need my services and feel guilty about it. Besides, I seldom have time to enjoy the results of my labor. There's no charity in my offer. The work is often hard physically and sometimes emotionally draining. You'll earn your keep."

Suddenly it was impossible for her to resist any longer. She felt the prickle of happy tears. Unable to thank him, fearing the tears would flow out of control, she said, "When do I report, boss? Your intelligent, educated, talented partner can't legally practice her profession at this time. She's run afoul of the law."

His brows knitted, admonishing her. "Picky, picky, picky."

He motioned with his head. "In the back, inside my coat pocket. I have a letter for you. I spent most of the morning getting people on the stick. I called a panel of DBA members, explained your problem and persuaded them to agree on a month's probation. The probation began the day you were suspended. Macomber was the tough one, but he finally gave in and agreed. Can you accept it?"

"You had a busy morning, didn't you?" Feeling awkward and on the spot, she reached for her hair and twisted an errant blonde curl. "Thanks, partner." She smiled broadly showing her even white teeth. "What a relief to realize it's all over."

"Don't thank me, just take me to bed again and make love to me."

She wiggled under the pressure of his stare. "Is sex your fee?"

"The best kind, in this case," he declared.

Mitch held her hand as the clouds beneath them disappeared. The terrain grew barren and forbidding. Soon they would be in Vegas. After her shaky beginning, she thought she could stay in his plane forever. He puzzled her. How could he do so much for her and not love her? Of course he loved her. He'd completely reversed his attitude regarding her career. Offering the partnership demonstrated it. Not so long ago, he was, to put it mildly, sarcastic about her work. He must love her. He had to. No longer doubting he loved her, Erika prayed for the patience to wait until she heard him say, "Erika, I love you." She watched the sky, hoping he wouldn't take too long.

# Chapter Twelve

AS SOON AS they had rented a car and left the airport, they drove directly to an exclusive dress salon in a local shopping center. Seated in comfortable chairs while a stylish woman brought several selections for their approval, Erika said. "How'd you know about this place?"

"I knew it might come to this, so Grayson told me about it when I called to accept his invitation. His wife shops here."

She felt bewildered and assumed she looked it. "I don't know," she murmured as the woman draped a slinky black dress over the table before them. "I was thinking about something pastel."

"Be right back," the woman said and disappeared with a flourish.

Erika reached for Mitch's hand. "Did you like any of them?"

He shook his head. "They were dreadful. I'm relieved to know you didn't care for them." A young lady in an extremely short skirt arrived and offered them a drink. Mitch accepted a glass of champagne and Erika refused, eying him disapprovingly. His eyes twinkled over the rim of his glass and he drank, watching her.

"I wish we hadn't come here. I'd prefer a rack of dresses where I could choose what I think I would like."

"Courage," he remarked. "The mechanical doll is returning." Erika looked up to see their salesperson returning. Mitch was right. She looked like a large doll, almost unreal in her outrageous dress. Twenty minutes passed as the procedure was repeated. "Hmmm. I like this one," Mitch said, touching a lacey beige dress. The doll held it in front of her and began to talk. Erika tuned her out. It was a gorgeous dress, but the neckline plunged so far she'd never have the courage to wear it. Recovering from her dismay, Erika saw a jacket to fit over the revealing neckline when the occasion called for more modesty. "I like it," she said interrupting the woman's chatter.

Approximately an hour later, they left with her outfitted from head to toe and underneath. The total cost: more than her monthly salary. Speechless, she walked to the Mercedes Mitch rented, wishing for the Bronco. The process of making the purchases made her feel dowdy and embarrassed. Her humor didn't improve when they came close to a scene over her insistence on paying for the clothes. For once, Mitch had backed off, and she used a charge card. Not yet totally accustomed to her new mode of living, her hand shook when she signed for the purchase.

Erika was still in shock when they were ushered into a suite of rooms at their hotel: a sitting room, two bedrooms and two baths. "Choose the bath you want," he said before she could look around.

Her tight lips answered. "It doesn't matter."

He hung her dress on a nearby hanger. "Since it doesn't take me long to get ready, you start your shower, and I'll go buy our host and hostess a gift." He looked longingly at the dress. "I can't wait to see you in it. This is a three-S dress: sleek, simple and slinky. Why wouldn't you model it for me at the shop?"

She blushed. "I just wanted to get out of the place as quickly as I could."

He took her in his arms and cuddled to her. "It wasn't so bad."

"It was for me," she pouted.

He stroked her hair. "You'll be better after a shower." He gave her a friendly squeeze. "You'll drive everyone crazy in that dress."

She attempted to pull away, but couldn't. "I plan to wear the jacket."

Both his hands caressed her back. "What a shame!"

Pushing away, she picked up her bag, placed it on a table and opened it. She found a plastic envelope of cosmetics. "I'd better have my shower now."

"And I'll go buy a gift." He seemed reluctant to go and she watched him eying her as she brushed past him, headed for the shower.

In the bathroom, she thought she heard him on the phone before she turned on the water. She stepped inside the shower, offering her face and body to the sting of the spray. The feeling that she had failed a test at the dress salon aggravated her, and she began to review the problem to discover where she went wrong.

Erika drew in a sharp breath of pleasure when Mitch opened the shower door and lifted her out. He carried her to one of the beds and laid her on it gently. The tensions of the day wafted away when his mouth found hers. She closed her eyes and her lips parted eagerly, inviting his heated kiss.

Later, she lay in his arms, feeling delicious and exhausted. Leaning on his elbow and watching her as he spoke, his face shone with sensuous satisfaction. "Will you wear the dress without a jacket now?"

She rolled her head away and laughed quietly. "Some of the time," she told him.

"We're going to be late, but it was worth it," he said wearily and left. Before she returned to the shower, she languished in bed, listening to him whistle as he prepared to shower.

Almost two hours later, they were hopelessly lost somewhere west of Las Vegas. Eventually, Mitch stopped to ask for directions, reluctance showing in every bone as he climbed out of the car. When he returned, he looked so chastened, Erika stifled the impulse to tease him. He sighed, "I just hate asking directions. They either treat you like a lost child or they don't know any more about where you're going than you do."

He was so serious, she didn't dare laugh. "Which was this?" she bit her lip to keep from smiling.

"Lost child. But I know the way now; it's going to take us a while more and we're late, late."

Erika looked at the elegantly wrapped package in her lap as he drove back onto the road. "I wish we knew what was in here."

"Don't worry," he chuckled. "We can fake it. I thought I was in luck. Not too many hotels have a shopping service." He glanced at her and winked. "It gave us a little extra time, and we used it in the best possible manner."

"But what if . . ."

"No what-ifs," he interjected, and then defended his actions. "The gift is probably better and more appropriate than what I'd buy."

Erika thought he missed the point of her concern. "Not telling them what you wanted to buy was a mistake. You're usually more careful. You don't want to be embarrassed. It may be something that . . ."

His voice was sharp. "Let's just drop it, OK?"

Mouth open and ready to continue, she sat a moment and let it go. The gift wasn't worth a fight. Minutes later, she stroked her dress. "It really is special, isn't it?"

"What's special?"

"The dress. It feels good next to my skin." He groaned audibly. "Once in a while, I've wondered how it would feel to wear expensive clothes like this. Now I know."

He stroked her knee, apparently over his temper flare. "You can know how they feel from now on, partner."

"Did you see my hand shake when I signed for the clothes this afternoon?" She laughed. "My new lifestyle will take some getting used to."

"You're already adjusting. A small tremor in the hand instead of panic is a good beginning."

Erika held up the package, straightening the bow. "I'm happy about the partnership."

"I know."

She frowned. "How did I get mixed up with an arrogant, cocksure defense attorney?"

"I'm convinced you're lucky."

How could she argue with his answer? "Right," she said, "I am."

They turned off the highway and the Mercedes crawled slowly up a dusty road to the top of a hill where a colonial-style mansion sat regally.

"This friend of yours does very well," she remarked, as he helped her from the car. "He has an indecently large house."

"Ken does all right." His remark was terse and he looked nervous. "But I never understood him wanting to live in Nevada."

She heard the edge in his voice. "Is something wrong?"

"I hope not," he replied.

As they crossed the porch, a man opened the door for them, beaming. He was taller than Mitch and much thinner. She thought his white hair was very distinguished. "Mitch, we expected you almost two hours ago. Where have you been? We were about to organize a posse and come looking for you."

"Lost in the desert. I'm sorry, Ken."

She watched as they shook hands. "And this must be Erika," Ken said and took her hand. I'm Ken Grayson. Please come in. Chances are you won't know a soul here, but do the best you can until I find Marsha. Just walk through to the back and you'll find the bar near the pool. Marsha and I will be right with you."

After he left, Erika said, "You didn't give him the gift."

"I forgot, and now I have cold feet. I'll tell him to expect something to be delivered tomorrow." Mitch took the package and tucked it behind a plant as they walked through the house. "I'll pick it up later when we leave." Outside, he fetched the drinks as she looked around the pool area and mentally counted the people.

"There must be fifty people here."

"At least," he agreed and gulped his drink with apparent satisfaction.

Her eyes wandered to the well-dressed women. "I'm glad I bought this dress. You were right. Jeans aren't in style tonight. There's a lot of money on the backs of these people."

They exchanged small talk and watched the other guests until Grayson found them. He was accompanied by his wife. Marsha Grayson's eyes gleamed during the introductions, and Erika couldn't believe she'd found her gorgeous blue dress in the shop they visited earlier. "Welcome," she said. "If you two can wait just a few minutes longer, we'll be right with you." She tugged at her husband's arm. "Ken, let's use the study. No one's in there."

"Good idea, dear," Ken said as she walked away and winked at Mitch. "Your Erika is a handsome woman. You always were lucky with the ladies." He spoke to Erika. "You're welcome to join us afterwards if you wish, but if you leave quickly, we'll understand. Now please excuse us and we'll get this group eating. Give us about twenty minutes, and we'll meet you in the study." Before Erika could ask what was going on, Grayson stepped up on a small retaining wall. "Ladies and gentlemen," he called. "The buffet is ready in the dining room. Won't you join us inside?" The crowd drifted toward the house and Erika waited not so patiently to discover what was happening.

Mitch led her inside. He spoke to one of the servants. "Where's the study?" They followed the directions given, opened the door and slipped inside.

"I'm hungry," Erika said. "I'd rather eat."

"I'll buy you dinner later." His eyes shifted to the door. "I'll take you to McDonald's and settle my bet. OK?"

"What's bothering you?" she demanded.

"Nothing." Now Mitch appeared genuinely nervous. His expression told her he felt insecure, a decidedly new look for him. He shifted his weight forward and muttered something. Moving to her, he held her close, "Erika, I love you. Will you marry me?"

A numb moment passed swiftly. She pulled away from him. "Say what you just said again."

"Whew," he breathed. "The next step will be a witness to testify to my words." He stood very straight. "I love you, Erika Wheatly. Will you marry me?"

"I knew you loved me, I knew it," she squealed. Melting to him, she whispered, "I love you." Unabashed, she made no attempt to hide her joy. "You've made me very happy, counselor."

"Will you marry me?" He asked cautiously.

Her arms twined around his neck and she snuggled tightly against him. "When you decide to make a move, you move swiftly don't you?" She hugged him warmly and muttered, "I'll marry you. Anywhere, anytime." She moved her head to look at him. "You're probably going to tell me we're going to be married tonight."

He nodded. "Any minute now."

"I can't wait," she whispered. "But we can't be married any minute now. We may never find our way back to town."

"Cheap shot, Erika. Correct, but cheap." He rocked her gently before he spoke. "Ken is a judge. Because we're friends, he agreed to marry us tonight, even if he's having an anniversary party."

Slightly flushed and with a glint of amusement, Erika planted a kiss on his lips. "You're beautiful," she said before stepping back. "We weren't invited to this party, were we?"

He nodded his head. "Yes, we were. You heard him invite us." He grinned sheepishly. "We were supposed to be here and married before the party started."

She laughed. "Is it their anniversary?"

"It's an anniversary party, but the real occasion takes place Sunday."

Erika fell into his arms laughing. She pushed away from him. "There are hundreds of wedding chapels around. We could have gotten married in one of those. It's too bad to cause your friend all this trouble."

Mitch pulled her to him roughly. "Ken doesn't care, and isn't this better than a dreary wedding chapel?" He kissed her again. "Besides, I know Ken's a judge and the marriage will be legal and binding."

Erika snuggled, molding herself to him. "Why didn't you tell me you planned our wedding?"

"I didn't want you to have a chance to back out."

"You knew I wouldn't back out. Seriously, Mitch, why?"

"Nothing serious about it. The look on your face when you're happy with a surprise is worth a month of scheming."

She tightened her arms about him. "I like your surprises, counselor." She nuzzled his neck fondly. "Tell me, when did you decide you loved me?"

"Months ago in a dull gray hallway. I fell victim to love at first sight."

"You can't mean that?"

"Oh, yes," he replied. "I haven't been the same since that day."

"Then what took you so long to tell me?"

"I knew you'd ask. It's tough to explain. I'll sound like an insensitive ogre."

"Try," she said quietly.

Mitch frowned and sighed. "I'd rather skip it. Can't I explain later?" Erika shook her head. He shifted around, resembling a nervous child hoping for a reprieve.

"Go on," she urged.

He gritted his teeth and began. "I was completely satisfied with my life when you breezed in with those big blue eyes and shapely legs, and for me, it was instant attraction. After our first date, I knew I had a problem. My life was never going to be the same, and I was right about that. I wasn't prepared for a significant other messing me up."

Erika almost choked. She had felt he intruded in her well-planned life, and he had felt the same way about her. She tried to interrupt.

"Quiet. I'm on a roll," he said and kissed the tip of her nose. "Admittedly, competing with your profession aggravated me, but I was wrong about your work. If you want a career, you have the right to it and I can live with that. It wasn't easy to leave you, but it was impossible to get you out of my mind. By the time I returned, I was determined to marry you, but my stubborn pride got in the way and I accepted Josh's case." He shook his head in disbelief. "Biggest mistake I ever made, taking that case. It didn't occur to me until later, I let my work come between us. I browbeat you for letting your job trespass in our lives, then I turn around and do the same thing. With my rash and impulsive nature, I could have lost you."

Her lips curled into a small smile. "Would you believe I decided it was time for me to take some chances and tell you I loved you? Kinda give you a shove so you'd speak up?"

He rolled his head back and roared, "We've simply got to do something to improve our timing."

"Your offer of the law partnership? Was it only a concession?"

"Not entirely. I couldn't have a more loyal partner, could I? If you're half as loyal to our clients as you were to the DA's office, and Rick, and even to Josh, you'll be a great defense attorney. Besides, I'll have you where I want you: with me."

There was no describing how she felt. She bent her head to his shoulder for a moment, savoring the feeling. He pushed her back and looked at her lovingly. "There was no way we were going to leave Las Vegas without being married."

She posed with her hands on her hips. "That sure of me, huh?"

"Yup," he answered and squeezed her hard.

Suddenly, she jumped back speaking in her hoarse voice. "Oh, Mitch. What are we going to use for a ring?"

He patted his coat pocket. "Don't worry. I thought of everything." Erika kissed him, giddy with happiness.

"You have no idea how happy I feel."

"Maybe not, but I'm experiencing some twinges of joy myself. It's not every day I get a wife and a new business partner."

Twenty minutes later, Mitch fished the gift from behind the plant where it was stashed. "Here's your wedding gift, Mrs. Logan. I hope you like it?"

With a pretense of being coy, she fluttered her eyelashes innocently. "For me? Whatever could it be?"

"Who knows, or cares?" he said through his laughter.